PRAISE FOR SIMON BRETT AND THE CHARLES PARIS SERIES

"Brett views the theater world with affectionate humor. He can be wickedly witty when he takes aim at some of its absurdities and pretensions."

—*Washington Post*

"What gives the series its continuing appeal is Brett's eye and ear for the world of acting [in any medium]."

—*Los Angeles Times*

"[Brett] has produced an insider's view of a complicated, charming, sordid and shoddy world, but always with comedic wit and pinpoint timing. His characters are appallingly human and appealingly drawn."

—*Dallas Morning News*

"Paris is probably crime fiction's most complex and developed series character."

—*Chicago Sun Times*

"Charles Paris is a refreshment and a delight."

—*San Francisco Examiner*

Corporate Bodies

SIMON BRETT

W❂RLDWIDE®

TORONTO • NEW YORK • LONDON
AMSTERDAM • PARIS • SYDNEY • HAMBURG
STOCKHOLM • ATHENS • TOKYO • MILAN
MADRID • WARSAW • BUDAPEST • AUCKLAND

CORPORATE BODIES

A Worldwide Mystery/October 1993

This edition is reprinted by arrangement with Charles Scribner's Sons; an imprint of Macmillan Publishing Company.

ISBN 0-373-26130-6

To Roger and Hilary

ONE

ONE OF THE REASONS why I became an actor, Charles Paris reflected wryly as he swung the wheel of the forklift truck, was to avoid tedious jobs like this. To avoid any job in fact with a predictability about it, any job for which you had to turn up at the same predictable hour every day, in which you had to climb a predictable career structure, in anticipation of a predictable retirement age and a predictable pension.

Actually, when he came to think about it, he wouldn't have minded the predictable pension. Or the predictable salary, come to that. He'd survived more than thirty years of the actor's fluctuating fortunes—long periods of 'signing on' enlivened by occasional bouts of work—but it was a kind of insecurity into which he'd never quite relaxed. As he got older, he did fantasise increasingly, with a slight wistfulness, about the idea of a regular income. This shaming thought was not one that he'd have mentioned to a fellow-actor, but it was there, lurking.

Maybe if he'd had a regular job, he conjectured, with regular hours, a regular salary and regular promotion, his life might have had more shape. Maybe his marriage might even have stayed together. Though it was difficult to envisage Frances in the role of a corporate wife. Everything might have been better, though. It was hard to be sure.

On the other hand, it was extremely easy to be sure that any employment of that kind would have driven him mad with boredom.

Charles Paris was an actor, like it or not. Even when, as in some years, his earnings were too low to qualify for taxation; even when, as in slightly better years, the taxman had the nerve to hound him for a slice of the little he had; even when directors, blind to his obvious genius, callously turned him down for parts; even when critics advised him to take up market gardening (as *The Financial Times* once had); whatever disasters arose, Charles Paris's mind couldn't cope with the idea of being in any other profession.

And driving a forklift truck in the Delmoleen warehouse for a morning was quite fun. It was only the idea of having to do it every morning—and every afternoon, come to that—that was insufferably tedious.

He looked across at Trevor, who actually did have to do it every day. The operator looked sullen. His bad temper, however, was not caused by the eternal tedium of his job, but by the fact that that particular morning Charles Paris was doing it.

The trouble was that that morning the job involved *speaking* and while Trevor was a dab hand at forklifts, capable of performing pirouettes on a man-up orderpicker, or turning a narrow-aisle swivel-head reach-truck on a 5p piece to bring down a palletised ton's load stored twenty feet above his head, when it came to *speaking* he wasn't so hot. Which was why the company had brought in an actor to do the speaking for him.

Delmoleen was making a video to show at trade fairs, encourage recruitment and generally bolster company solidarity. Charles Paris had become involved in exactly the same way that he got most of his jobs—through a friend.

Charles did have an agent, but it often seemed that getting work for his clients was against Maurice Skellern's religion. Taking 15 per cent on the work they got for themselves was, however, quite within the Commandments, and Charles, who had set up the Delmoleen job direct, was anxious lest his agent should find out about it.

The friend who had introduced him to his first corporate video was called Will Parton, a writer whom Charles Paris had encountered on the *Stanislas Braid* television series. Will's destiny in life, as he kept telling anyone and everyone who would listen, was to write a major serious stage play. He'd had the idea for years, just a matter of carving out enough time actually to get the thing written.

But the creation of the *magnum opus* kept getting deferred by television work. 'Well, you have to pay the bills,' as Will kept saying with an apologetic shrug. In fact, for Will Parton, as a single man in a highly-paid profession living in a two-bedroom flat, the bills were not too daunting. He could easily have afforded a six-month sabbatical to get the play written—had he really had the will to do it.

But he found television work so lucrative and—once he'd taken on board the fact that it involved more *re*writing than writing—so comparatively easy, that the serious stage play, like the horizon, constantly receded. Writing a corporate video for Delmoleen was, in spite of the way Will kept talking about 'taking on a new challenge' and 'broadening my range', simply another way of staving off the evil moment when he'd have to find out if his play idea really was any good.

But he wasn't involved just as a writer. Will Parton, perhaps in reaction to the countless years he had spent being ordered around by countless directors, had recently gone into production. He had formed a company called *Parton Parcel*, through which he hoped to dip his own ladle into the corporate gravy train. Though its impressive letterhead featured the names of various friends to give a bit of *gravitas*, the organisation was in fact a one-man band. Will reckoned to bring in other staff as and when required. When he got a production, he would hire in freelance directors, cameramen, soundmen and so on. There was no shortage of such skilled personnel around; the recession in television was biting everywhere.

The Delmoleen contract was the first that *Parton Parcel* had secured. Will had followed up a contact in the company, who had introduced him to the Delmoleen Marketing Director just at the moment when the Managing Director had expressed the need for a morale-boosting video. Will Parton had had a meeting with the Marketing Director, who knew nothing of that particular world, and produced the requisite bullshit, as a result of which the *Parton Parcel* tender, suitably modest for such a relatively new set-up, had been accepted.

Charles Paris had had no compunction about accepting Will's offer to put him up for the video. The writer had rung one evening and said, 'The Delmoleen people'll take you on my say-so, no problem. They don't know anything about actors.'

Deciding, as he usually did on such occasions, not to take offence at the inadvertent slight, Charles had responded enthusiastically. The previous few months had been, in Maurice Skellern's favourite phrase, 'quiet, very quiet'. In fact, the previous year had been almost totally silent, one of the worst of Charles's career. The rumbles of approaching recession had led to cutbacks in the theatre and advertising and, as the commercial companies began the ritual circling which precedes the award of new franchises, television opportunities had also become very limited. Things were always bad in his profession, but Charles had never known them quite this bad.

'What is Delmoleen?' he asked after Will had confirmed an interview time for the following day. 'Bedtime drink ... ?'

'Well, yes, Delmoleen "Bedtime" is the best known product in this country, but they manufacture a whole bundle of other stuff. All food products. You'd be amazed at the diversity, and the places they export to. I tell you, Charles, I've had to read so much guff on Delmoleen that I'm now one of the world's experts. I could bore you for hours on the subject.'

'Don't bother.'

'No, I'll leave that to the Delmoleen executives. God, they take it all so seriously. Make Muslim Fundamentalists look insipid ... Ooh, that is a thought. One thing, Charles ...'

'Yes?'

'*You* have to take it seriously too. No giggling.'

His voice took on a tone of injured innocence. 'Would I?'

'Won't even answer that. No, please, whatever crap they talk—and I can guarantee you they will talk plenty of crap—straight face, OK? And don't you dare catch my eye.'

'I will be as demure as a Jane Austen heroine.'

'Hm.' The writer didn't sound convinced.

'Oh, Will, what should I wear?'

'For the interview?'

'Right. In my experience of commercials and things, if you don't turn up in the right gear, you don't get the part.'

'Yes, it'll be just the same with this lot. They haven't got the imagination to realise that an actor's capable of wearing different clothes.' Will dropped into the drawl of a theatrical pseud. 'OK, love, the major role you are being considered for in my new *oeuvre* is that of... a forklift truck driver.'

'*A forklift truck driver?*' Charles echoed in his best Lady Bracknell. 'I don't believe I am familiar with the customary garb of forklift truck drivers.'

'Well, if you follow the sartorial style of Trevor, who is one of the real ones on-site, you'll go for a tasteful Status Quo T-shirt, a pair of appropriately understated tracksuit bottoms and rather grubby trainers.'

Charles moved into his Victorian actor-manager voice. 'I will obtain the requisite wardrobe. And vocally...? I dare say a person in such employment would favour the vowels of the proletariat...?'

'Yes, better be a bit "off".'

'It shall be done.'

'OK, Charles, see you tomorrow. Train to Bedford, change there on to the branch line to Stanley Curton. Factory's just opposite the station. Go to main reception, ask for Ken Colebourne's office.'

'Right. Thanks for putting my name up.'

'No problem. But remember—don't giggle!'

THE AUDITION—no, he must stop saying that, it gave away how long he'd been in the business, no actor younger than Charles Paris ever used the word 'audition', they all talked about 'interviews' these days—the *interview* for the Delmoleen job was not the most artistically taxing that he had ever undergone.

As any actor should, he had of course prepared for the encounter to come, trying out voices and expressions in front of his mirror, and taking on the character with its tracksuit, T-shirt and trainers. (It was a mild May. He didn't need any kind of topcoat.)

For the train to Bedford, he had even gone to the extent of buying a copy of the *Sun* rather than his customary *Times*. Unfortunately, having read every word of the paper twice before the train drew out of St Pancras, he was reduced to looking out of the window for the rest of his journey. Still, he comforted himself, that is probably what a forklift truck driver would have done, so, boring though it might be, he was at least continuing to get into character.

He reflected that, to go the whole hog, he should really have got into a 'Smoking' compartment and lit up a Players Number Six, but there were some things, even for his art, Charles Paris could not bring himself to do.

Will Parton's directions had been precise and Charles found his way to the Delmoleen site without any hitches. The view from the exit to Stenley Curton railway station was dominated by a long two-storey brick building directly opposite. Probably late nineteenth century, it had been built for some unspecified and discontinued industrial purpose, but now unmistakably belonged to Delmoleen. The company logo arched hugely over the main gates, and reappeared on the new fascia that had been grafted on to the reception area.

When Charles asked for Ken Colebourne, he was directed out of the main building to the township of low modern rectangles behind. Though these looked boring and functional from the outside, the interior of the office into which he was ushered was anonymously graceful, with black wood and smoked glass, low tables, charcoal sofas and armchairs. Expensively photographed and discreetly framed Delmoleen products looked down from the walls.

Will was already there, and introduced the other two men. The writer was dressed in a voluminous suit and exotic tie, a marked contrast from his customary uniform of denim shirt and jeans. 'They don't listen to you if you're not wearing a suit,' he had confided. 'Always got to go for the *gravitas* in this business, you know, Charles.'

Charles was invited to sink into one of the sofas. Coffee was produced. He sat there, waiting to be asked to do his bit, but Ken Colebourne, the Marketing Director, and Robin Pritchard, the Product Manager for Biscuits and Cereals, showed no interest at all in his artistic abilities.

This was probably just as well. On the phone the night before, Charles and Will Parton had spun some childish fantasies about suitable audition pieces for the meaty role under consideration.

Charles had opened the bidding rather feebly with 'To lift or not to lift, that is the question'. Then Will had gone all Keatsian with a reference to 'bursting Joy's grape against his pallet fine'. Charles had countered by 'Once more unto the reach-truck, friends, once more/Or fill the shelves up with unwanted stock'; after which their conversation had degenerated into a series of variations on the word 'fork', until Charles ended things by saying that such jokes were terribly vulgar and 'the kind of thing with which he would no longer have any truck'.

The result of all this was that, if he had been asked to read anything, the giggle-risk-factor might have become unacceptably high. Being in costume and character, as always, reduced the danger, but didn't eliminate it completely. Still, so long as he didn't catch Will's eye, Charles found he could look appropriately and soberly impressed while Ken Colebourne expatiated on the many virtues of the Delmoleen company and products.

'I mean, we are very big. And when I say big, I mean *big*. Isn't that right, Robin?'

'Oh yes, Ken. Delmoleen is *big*.'

'I mean, still an independent corporation, we haven't been swallowed up into one of the multinationals, but the fact remains that our outreach is *big*.'

'*Global*,' Robin Pritchard confirmed, '*global*.'

'Ah. Right. Good,' said Charles, in his enthusiastic but slightly non-committal 'off' voice. Actually, it was the one he had used in *The Birthday Party* at Bury St Edmunds ('Charles Paris's performance seemed nearer to Panto than Pinter'—*Eastern Daily Press*).

'But, though we're big,' Ken Colebourne went on, 'we are still a *caring* company. Caring for the environment, obviously... Isn't that right, Robin?'

'Right, Ken.'

'But also caring for our employees. And that's what this video's about. It's to show that everyone the company employs is part of the Delmoleen family, and that "big" doesn't automatically mean impersonal.'

The pause extended. Charles, reminding himself he wasn't back in *The Birthday Party*, broke the silence with a 'Right'.

'This is something that's a big priority with B.T.'

'Right,' said Charles again, wondering mildly what British Telecom had to do with food products.

'He's very much behind the whole concept.'

Clocking the fact that 'B.T.' was a person, Charles threw in a 'Good' by way of variety.

'Isn't that right, Robin?'

'Oh, certainly, Ken. The whole thing's really Brian's baby.'

So that sorted out the 'B' of 'B.T.' Brian who? Clearly someone of considerable importance in the hierarchy. Charles nodded thoughtfully, deciding that, given the awe with which the name had been mentioned, it would be inappropriate to ask who 'B.T.' or 'Brian' was.

He wondered if the difference in the way the two men spoke of their superior was another reflection of the difference in their styles. 'B.T.' had a dated and distanced feel to it, while the 'Brian' implied not only a more informal approach, but also greater intimacy in the Product Manager's relationship.

'And you've always been the midwife to Brian's babies, haven't you, Ken?'

As Robin Pritchard said this, Charles was aware of an undercurrent in the younger man's voice. It was nothing as positive as insolence, but the intonation implied some kind of challenge. And a flicker in the Marketing Director's expression showed that he was aware of that challenge.

They were a contrasted pair; Ken Colebourne short and thick-set, grey-haired but with eyebrows and moustache still black. The suit was bluish with close white stripes: the tie, red blue and white bands of different widths that didn't quite amount to anything regimental. Ken's voice had a Midland roughness. He gave the impression of a tough pragmatist who had worked up the hard way. Not a man with a great sense of humour. Certainly not a man to cross.

The Product Manager for Biscuits and Cereals was at least twenty years younger, and had more obvious educational gloss. University certainly, possibly business school as well. The brown suit on his long frame was more fashionably floppy than Ken Colebourne's, the tie looked like a detail from some twentieth-century abstract painting. Robin Pritchard wore round tortoiseshell glasses, and had either a weak mouth or a permanently sardonic expression. Or possibly both.

Suddenly Charles identified the quality in the younger man's voice. Robin Pritchard was, ever so slightly, sending up Ken Colebourne. His older colleague was fully aware of this, and didn't like it. Ken was the one who was meant to be running the interview, but Robin very subtly implied that it was taking place by his licence.

'The reason we wanted to see you, Mr Paris...' the Marketing Director went on. 'I mean, obviously we respect Will's advice and his recommendation of you as an actor...but we had to check that you look right.'

'Right,' Charles echoed reasonably.

'You see, this video will be seen all over the place. I mean, in-house, as induction to new employees...quite possibly for recruitment purposes... probably at trade fairs... It is going to cover the whole international scope of the Delmoleen operation—and that is *big*, as I may have said.'

Yes, thought Charles, you *have* said it. A few times.

'So, it's important that we don't have anyone in the video who looks wrong for the Delmoleen image.'

'No, we do have a *global* profile to maintain, after all, don't we, Ken?' Now that Charles had identified the element of mockery in Robin Pritchard's manner, it seemed more overt.

As intended, the Marketing Director was a little flustered. 'Yes, yes, of course. So, really, Mr Paris, we've called you in just to have a look at you, see how you fit in to the Delmoleen picture.'

'Well, here I am,' said Charles, spreading his arms wide in an ingenuous shrug.

'Yes...yes...' said Ken Colebourne, focusing on the actor as if for the first time, as though he hadn't been able to form any visual impressions while he'd been talking. After a moment's scrutiny, there was another thoughtful 'Yes'; then another; then 'I'm not really too sure...'

'Oh, for heaven's sake, Ken. You're not at a cattle market.' Robin Pritchard turned to Charles with confidential bonhomie. 'I do apologise for my colleague's bad manners, Mr Paris.'

'No problem.' And it wasn't. Compared to the diplomatic skills demonstrated by some television directors, this was the height of good manners.

Robin Pritchard's words were a problem for Ken Colebourne, however. Again, the Marketing Director had winced, biting back some angry riposte. He knew that, in a verbal contest, the younger man would be the more nimble and only make him look clumsy.

'To be quite frank, Robin, I'm a bit worried about the age factor...'

Charles tried not to show that the barb had been hurtful. Like all actors, he always tried to look younger than his real age. This was not—or at least not wholly—for the reasons of vanity that drive some women to such deceptions; it was a matter of simple survival. There are few enough parts around, anyway; no actor wants to disqualify himself from any of them by being too old. Whenever Charles was asked at an audition—sorry, interview—the direct question, 'How old are you?', his automatic reply was, 'Forty-eight, but play younger.' Which wasn't the exact truth, but near enough for an actor.

Ken Colebourne expanded his point. 'I mean, remember, what B.T.'s keen to do is to project the overall image of Delmoleen. Is that going to be helped by having a forklift truck driver on the verge of retirement?'

Ouch! Now that one really did hurt.

Will Parton came to his friend's rescue. 'The point is, Ken, that we want to project the *whole* company... you know, like an extended family. So we've got to have a spread of ages. I mean, the kid who's going to be in the office for this warehouse sequence, Dayna, is only about eighteen... but we need the other end of the spectrum too. In an extended family, you've got kids... and you've got grandfathers...'

How dare you, Will? Even though he was a grandfather three times over, Charles Paris wasn't enjoying the direction of the conversation one bit.

'I'm still not sure...'

Will came in with the clincher. 'Brian was very keen on this when I talked to him. I mentioned the "extended family" idea and he liked it a lot.'

'Oh. Oh well, that's fine then. Consider yourself hired, Mr Paris.'

Ken Colebourne reached a stubby hand across his desk. Robin Pritchard seemed to find something infinitely amusing in a vortex at the end of his tie. Will Parton looked innocently up to the ceiling. Charles Paris tried to avoid his friend's eye.

And that's how he got the job of being a forklift truck driver.

TWO

'No, no, no, no!' said Trevor. 'You got to swing the wheel round with more power than that.'

'Well, I don't want to go crashing into—' Charles began.

'I thought that looked fine, actually,' the director, Griff Merricks, interposed in a conciliatory tone. Not difficult for him; conciliatory was the only tone he possessed.

Now over sixty, Griff's main claim to fame in the business was his 'unflappability'. Charles suspected that this quality, which at times verged on torpor, arose from the fact that the director had no interest whatsoever in any of the work he did. He was a competent framer of shots, unimpeded by imagination, who had pottered along amiably enough in the BBC until he reached retirement age, and was therefore now ideally qualified to direct corporate videos.

Will Parton, having worked with Griff on a few projects and knowing him to be 'safe' to the point of tedium, had offered him the Delmoleen job on behalf of *Parton Parcel*. Glad once again to be in work, Griff Merricks continued as he always had done, resolutely safeguarding apple-carts from the risk of upset.

Trevor the forklift driver, however, seemed bent on a rampage of apple-cart upsetting. At the beginning of the morning he had been most amenable, keen to show off his forklifting skills and demonstrating a lively in-

terest in the camera that was being used for the filming ('Like, a bit of a hobby of mine, video, like...').

In fact, he had been perfectly docile until he discovered what Charles's role was to be in the proceedings. From that moment, he had made as much
trouble as he could. And was clearly not about to
change his behaviour.

'It didn't bloody look fine!' he protested. 'Listen,
I've done the tricky bit on the truck, haven't I? I ac-
tually brought the pallet down from the shelves, didn't
I?'

'Yes,' Griff Merricks conceded soothingly. 'But
when we filmed that, we did it in longshot. What we're
doing now is cutting to Charles in close-up to say the
lines. All we need to see from him on the truck is the
final turn of the steering wheel.'

'But what I'm saying is that the people watching this
video's going to think that he and me're the same person.'

'Yes, that's the idea.'

'That's why you've put us in these bleeding overalls, isn't it?'

Trevor pulled disparagingly at the pristine blue
fabric. Charles looked down at his overalls, thinking
of all the wasted effort he'd put into matching Trev-
or's usual costume. He caught the eye of Will Parton,
who was clearly thinking the same thing. The writer
smugly preened in his neat suit and tie. Charles looked
abruptly away. If he started giggling now, the aggrieved Trevor was quite likely to assume the laughter
was at his expense and become even more belligerent.

'Well, it's partly that, Trevor,' Griff Merricks was
agreeing tactfully, '—so that you and Charles look

alike—but it's also because the overalls have got the Delmoleen logo on them, and throughout the film Ken's very keen to build up the corporate identity, so that whenever we see one of the workers—I mean, a Delmoleen employee other than a management executive—we see them wearing these overalls.'

'But nobody in the company actually does wear them.'

'No, Trevor, but for the video they do.'

'Huh. Right load of cobblers this video's going to be then, isn't it?'

'We-ell . . .'

Charles's gaze wandered round the warehouse. It was a massive space, divided into sections by high walls of shelving loaded with pallets of Delmoleen products. Other yellow forklift trucks lay idle in the narrow aisles. The shutters of the loading bays along one wall were open, showing the maws of empty lorries. At one end of the space were offices, two prefabricated structures, stacked on top of each other like shoeboxes against the wall.

It felt strange to be working there. Not that Charles hadn't worked in stranger settings, but that had always been for drama, when all the resources of the location had been dedicated to the production. In this case, the priorities were different, and the film crew was clearly a positive hindrance to the main business of the warehouse.

Still, Trevor seemed impervious to the resentment of his workmates and was in no mood to expedite the morning's shoot. 'Point I'm making is, if you have *him*'—a contemptuous finger was jerked towards Charles—'turning the wheel of the truck like a wanker, people who see it're going to think I'm a wanker, aren't they?'

'It's a point of view...' Griff Merricks looked nonplussed. Maybe conciliation wasn't going to be enough in this particular case; unfortunately it was the only weapon his armoury contained.

Charles stepped into the breach. 'Look, Trevor, perhaps you could show me again how to do it,' he humbly suggested, vacating the driver's seat. 'You do it so well, and I know I'm making a real pig's breakfast of it.'

'You can bloody say that again,' Trevor concurred. But the simple psychology had worked; it had brought a grin—albeit a patronising one—to the driver's face. He sprang into the truck's seat with insulting ease.

'Look, can we make it quick, please...?' This wingeing voice belonged to Alan Hibbert, the Warehouse Manager, who had been hovering around uneasily all morning, trying time and again to move the proceedings along.

He had received assurances from Ken Colebourne that the filming would only take a couple of hours and would cause minimum disruption. Unversed in the ways of television and film—where everything always takes immeasurably longer than it's meant to and where the words 'minimum disruption' always mean 'maximum disruption'—Alan Hibbert had actually believed the Marketing Director's words. And was now, to his cost, finding out the truth.

Ken Colebourne had kept saying that they were only using one aisle for the filming and that the work of the rest of the warehouse could continue uninterrupted, but every time Alan Hibbert tried to get one of the other forklifts going, it either became entangled in the spaghetti of cables spawned by the cameras and lights or was ordered to stop because it was making too much noise during a take.

The marriage between show business and the industrial process were not getting off to a very good start.

'Look, it's dead simple. Bloody child of three could do it.'

Charles grinned weakly, prepared to suffer Trevor's scorn in the cause of speed.

'First you switch on the ignition—right?'

Charles, nodding like an idiot, watched the key turned, as if the operation were a complex feat of microsurgery. 'Right.'

'And then you simply push this lever on the left of the steering wheel forward and you're in gear—right?'

Charles watched his manoeuvre completed with the ardour of Galahad being given a sneak preview of the Holy Grail. 'Right. You don't use the clutch?' he asked breathlessly.

'Can do, but don't have to,' Trevor assured him. 'And look—you're moving.'

'So you are,' agreed Charles, amazed by the miracle of the forklift truck slowly edging forwards.

'And then you give it a touch of the accelerator to go faster.'

'Just like a car, really.'

This thought did not seem to have struck Trevor before. 'Well, yeah, I suppose, if you like. Bit like a car.'

On reflection, he decided this comparison might diminish the mystery of his calling. 'Different from a car, though.'

'Yes, of course.'

'I mean, driving a forklift . . . well, it's a specialised skill.'

'I'll say.'

Trevor flashed a look at Charles, suspecting mockery. Unable to decide whether or not there had been any, he went on, 'Anyway, what you got to do is swing the wheel like *so*.' He matched the action to his words. 'With a bit of bloody beef, though. If people are going to think it's me, I don't want to come across as a bleeding fairy, do I?'

This prompted a laugh from somewhere over behind the stacks. Trevor turned sharply at the sound but could not identify its source.

'No. Right,' said Charles, long accustomed to the fact that 50 per cent of the population thought all actors were 'bleeding fairies'. Presumably, it had been one of that 50 per cent who had just laughed.

'Reckon you can do that then?' Trevor asked, his voice again heavy with sarcasm.

'Think so.' Charles judiciously mixed humility into the confidence of his reply.

Trevor didn't look convinced. He nonchalantly swung the wheel of the forklift again and brought the truck to rest exactly where it had started.

'That's terrific,' said Griff Merricks. 'Thank you very much, Trevor. Right, Charles, could we run it?'

But the real operator wasn't going to relinquish his seat to any thespian surrogate quite so easily. 'You don't smoke, do you?' he asked Charles accusingly.

'No, I don't.'

'Oh.' Trevor couldn't keep the disappointment out of his voice. 'Only you mustn't smoke round one of these.'

'Well, I wouldn't, because I don't.'

'And the whole warehouse is a "No smoking" area, anyway, Trevor,' Alan Hibbert pointed out testily.

But the operator was not to be deflected from his narrative. 'Point is,' he continued, eyeing Charles beadily, 'some of these trucks run on Calor gas, and there's a risk of a leak and if you get a naked flame from a cigarette—'

'Yes, well, since, as I say, I don't smoke, and since this one I'm working on is actually powered by electricity, I don't see—'

'Bloke in a warehouse over Northampton,' Trevor continued inexorably, 'he had a crafty fag while he was driving one of the Calor ones... Whole thing went "woomph"... they was picking bits of him off the shelves for months.'

'Well, that sounds—'

'What you have to watch with the electrical ones,' Trevor went on, 'is that you don't leave them with the engine running. Flattens the batteries. Have to be recharged every night, you see. If there's one way to get yourself unpopular in a warehouse, it's to leave your engine running and flatten your battery.'

'Well, I'll certainly be careful not to—'

'And this machine's got a "Quick Release" button, and all...'

'Has it?'

'It's got a guard over it, so's you can't push it by mistake...' Trevor appraised Charles disdainfully, 'well, unless you're a complete wanker. It's meant for lowering the forks quick when you've unloaded but, if you press it when you got a pallet up, whole sodding lot comes smashing down.'

'Ah,' said Charles, bewildered as to the cause of this sudden verbal diarrhoea. Maybe it was just intimidation, or perhaps the operator, affronted at the assumption that he wasn't up to the task of *speaking*, wanted to assert his credentials in that department.

Griff Merricks seemed to take the second view, or at least to reckon that it was Trevor's exclusion from a more active role in the filming that was making him so unco-operative. 'Um...' he proposed, 'I was wondering whether you would mind doing something else for me in the video...?'

'Oh?' The speed of reaction showed that the director had judged his subject right. There was a glint of enthusiasm in Trevor's grudging acquiescence. 'I suppose I could, if you insist—since my day's work's bloody shot to pieces, anyway.'

'Well, what I'd like you to do, Trevor, is to be seen chatting with the secretary who comes out of the warehouse office...'

'What do I say to her then?'

'It actually doesn't matter what you say. We won't hear it, just see you talking—OK?'

Trevor nodded magnanimously. 'Sure, I'll help you out.' He got down from the seat of the forklift. Granted another role in the proceedings, he no longer needed to continue asserting his dominance over Charles.

'So what I'd like to do now...' the director illustrated his intentions with wide arm movements, 'is pick up from the end of the manœuvre you just did for us, Trevor. We've got you bringing the pallet down at the end of the aisle—that's in the can. Then I want to sweep across the warehouse...'

'What, do a pan, like?' asked Trevor, keen to assert his mastery of video jargon.

'That's right—*pan* across the warehouse...and if you're walking towards the office, just as the secretary comes out...I'll linger for a moment on the two of you chatting...then come across to the end of the aisle...just as you're emerging on the forklift, Charles, and...' A thought crossed the director's mind. 'Is this going to be all right with you, Will?'

The writer, thus deferred to, shrugged his agreement. Serene in his suit, he was leaning against a pallet of Delmoleen 'Bedtime (Lite)' and being very accommodating about whatever changes to his script happened to be suggested. Like the video's director, he had had no creative interest at all in the filming. So long as *Parton Parcel* was being paid, so long as *Parton Parcel* paid him, and so long as nobody demanded any rewrites, he was quite content.

Even if he hadn't been a representative of the production company, the writer would still have been there for the shoot, maintaining at least the illusion of interest. And, Charles thought cynically, Will's attendance at Stenley Curton had the additional advantage of keeping him away from home. Stuck in his flat, he really would have no alternative but to start writing the definitive play.

'Then, Charles,' Griff went on, 'you say your bit and—'

'But how will I know when to walk and when to talk?' asked Trevor.

'I'll give you a cue.'

'A cue? What do I want a bleeding cue for?' The blank look on the operator's face suggested that he was thinking in terms of snooker. Perhaps interpreters, fluent in show business jargon, would be required.

'I'll give you a *wave*,' Griff Merricks hastily amended.

'Oh, right. So...what, you give Heather a wave and all, so's she knows when to come out...?'

'Yes. Though in fact it won't be Heather who gets the wave.'

'Why not? Heather's the only secretary round the warehouse. Runs the Dispatch Office—and don't we all know it? Real Miss Bossyboots, she is.'

'Yes, it's just we, um, we thought it might be better if we had someone else as the secretary.'

'Not bringing in another bleeding actor, are you? Actress, I should say.' Maliciously he added, 'If you can tell the difference.'

'No. No, it's someone from the company... Ah, here she is.'

The director turned to greet a young woman who had just entered the warehouse. Nature had made her pretty, and artifice had been enlisted to make her even prettier. Probably still only in her late teens, she had short blonde hair and big blue eyes emphasised by mascara-spiked lashes. A trim figure was outlined by her tiny navy business suit. The skirt, fashionably short, and the heels, fashionably high, showed her legs to advantage. The perfect picture was marred only by a discontented tightness round her thin lips.

'Ah, Dayna...' said Griff Merricks. 'Perfect timing. We were just getting to your bit. Dayna, this is Charles Paris.'

'Good morning, Dayna.'

'Hello.' She had the local accent, but there was a lethargic sexiness about her voice.

'And I don't know if you've met Trevor...'

It was clear from Trevor's expression, if not from Dayna's, that they certainly had met. In fact, the girl's arrival had reduced the operator to confusion. She offered him a cool grin, but he could only redden and stutter in response.

Suddenly further participation in the video seemed to have lost its appeal. 'Yeah, well, I think, actually, maybe I won't stick around. I'm on early dinners, so I think I'll, you know, be off...' And he walked out of the warehouse.

The girl watched him go without emotion, then turned the beam of her blue eyes on to Charles. A half-smile haunted her lips, waiting for a response from him. If he grinned, she would be prepared to laugh at the departing Trevor; if he gave her no encouragement, she wouldn't.

Charles gave nothing. The half-smile faded from her lips.

'Well, don't worry,' said Griff Merricks. 'I'm sure we can get one of the other operators to do that for us, can't we, Alan?'

'I'm sure we can,' the Warehouse Manager agreed sourly, 'particularly since they've been stopped all morning from doing bugger-all else.'

Another forklift truck operator was enlisted and issued with a new set of gleaming blue overalls. Charles sat in his truck and ran through the lines in his head. He tested out the machine, switching on the ignition and pushing forward the gear lever, which was very loose and engaged easily. The truck edged forward. Charles gave a little kick of acceleration and swung the steering wheel with what he hoped Trevor would consider sufficient beef.

The truck jerked sideways and the load on its fork crashed into a shelved pallet of Delmoleen 'Oat Nuggets'. Considering how relatively slowly he had been moving, the impact had caused quite a lot of damage, ripping the polythene covering and digging deep into the stacked cartons.

He looked around sheepishly, hoping no one had noticed, but was met by the unforgiving eye of Alan Hibbert. Charles tried to smile. 'Quite a powerful machine, isn't it?'

'Yes,' said the Warehouse Manager, tersely unamused. 'You just be bloody careful with it.'

'I will be.'

'And make sure it's bloody switched off when you've finished farting around with it.'

'Of course.'

Infinitely gentle, Charles reversed his truck away from the disaster and switched off the ignition. Trying to avoid Alan Hibbert's eye, he looked across to the ground-level office, inside which Griff Merricks was instructing Dayna on her first acting role. Behind them stood a dowdy woman of uncertain age. While Charles watched, she turned on her heel and went out of sight into another room. He wondered idly if the woman was Heather, the 'Miss Bossyboots' who ran the Dispatch Office.

THE LINES WERE NO PROBLEM, but a few takes were needed before Charles Paris could co-ordinate them perfectly with the movements of his forklift truck. Finally, on the fourth attempt, the timing worked.

As directed by Griff Merricks, the cameraman panned across the office end of the warehouse. On her cue, Dayna picked up an invoice from a desk and came out of the office, moving as if she hoped to be talent-stopped for a part in *Emanuelle XII*. The forklift truck operator who had replaced Trevor walked forward on his cue to meet her. They stopped and engaged in fascinated discussion about some detail of the invoice.

The camera panned across to the entrance of the aisle up which Charles Paris was gingerly coaxing his forklift truck. With aplomb, panache and—yes—beef, Charles swung the steering wheel round so that he was facing the camera, disengaged the gear lever, and launched into his speech. Will Parton's prose in this instance wasn't perhaps up to Pinter, but *The Birthday Party* voice still seemed to work fine.

'This is where many of the Delmoleen range of products get loaded to be transported to the four corners of the world. My job's an important part of the distribution process, and I get a lot of satisfaction from being a link in a global chain.' As instructed by Griff Merricks, Charles grinned and gave a little toss of his head. 'It's a good feeling to know that I'm a member of the Delmoleen family.'

Each time he said these words, Charles was again struck by the incongruity of a family which has to

book in actors to play its members, but he didn't let
this thought put him off the task for which he was being paid. Again following instructions, he engaged the
gear lever, swung the steering wheel round (with plenty
of beef), and drove the forklift truck sedately out of
shot.

Charles was surprised to hear a single pair of hands
clapping. As he looked round to the source of the
noise, it was quickly joined by the clapping of other
hands.

By the entrance to the warehouse was a little knot of
people. Ken Colebourne stood on one side, with Robin
Pritchard on the other, flanking a couple in the middle. The man, tall and fiftyish with a craggy face, wore
a dark suit and plain red tie; the woman, of about the
same age, was dressed in a pale blue suit, with co-
ordinated dark blue hat, shoes and handbag.

The craggy-faced man had been the first to clap.
The sycophantic speed with which the others had
joined him, and the nervous sheen on Ken Colebourne's forehead, left Charles in no doubt that the
newcomer was 'B.T.' or, as the more relaxed Robin
Prichard would call him, 'Brian'.

THREE

HIS NAME WAS Brian Tressider, and he was the Managing Director. The lady in pale blue was, predictably enough, his wife. She was called Brenda.

It was no surprise that their arrival caused a stir, but Charles felt the reaction was more than just one of awe. Brian Tressider was automatically impressive by virtue of his position, but he seemed also to command a great deal of affection amongst his workforce.

The warehouse staff gathered round him and he had a cheerful word and a Christian name for most of them. This wasn't just the researched 'common touch' of a politician; there seemed to be a genuine feeling among the employees that their MD was 'one of them'. Charles got the impression that Brian Tressider had worked his way up from the shop floor and was respected for it. The uneroded Midland twang in his voice supported that supposition.

His wife hadn't quite the same natural manner. Though she was punctiliously amiable and interested in everyone, Brenda Tressider's bonhomie showed signs of hard work—if not of calculation, then at least of application. Her vowels betrayed a more privileged upbringing than her husband's; she had the kind of upper-class voice which implies patronage and condescension even when they aren't there.

She must once have been beautiful and had since then been very well maintained. Her face now was lined beneath the skilful make-up and her hair had had an assisted passage towards blondeness, but the grey-blue eyes still packed a powerful punch. Charles also approved the suppleness of her well-exercised body. Quite classy.

He was introduced to both of them by an anxiously obsequious Ken Colebourne. The Marketing Director's cautious deference implied a less affable, steelier side to Brian Tressider, an insistence on high standards and a readiness to bawl out anyone who didn't match up to those standards.

Robin Pritchard was also watchful in his boss's presence. Though his manner was characteristically more laid-back than Ken's, the Product Manager was nonetheless on his best behaviour, ready to respond instantly to any switch in Brian's mood.

But that mood was currently sunny and looked set fair to remain so. Brian Tressider chatted easily to the people involved in the video, asking for technical explanations from Griff Merricks and his crew, joking with Will and Charles. If this was like a visit from royalty, it was a very relaxed one.

His wife's conversation, however, conformed to the more traditional royal style. 'Charles Paris? Yes, now of course I know the name. Tell me, what would I have seen you in recently?'

As ever, when asked this question, Charles's mind went a complete blank. Given the progress of his career during the previous year, a complete blank was entirely appropriate.

'Ah. Well, erm . . .'

'Of course, if it's theatre, we may not know as much about it as we should. Brian and I don't get to the theatre as often as we'd like these days. Do tend to get involved in quite a lot of evening functions.'

'Yes. Erm...' Suddenly, from the recesses of his memory, he dragged out a recollection of once having worked. 'I was in a television series that was on a couple of years back. Detective thing... *Stanislas Braid*... don't know if you, er...'

'Of course!' said Brenda Tressider. 'Of course, I knew I recognised the face.' This was phrased in such a way that she didn't have to admit whether or not she'd seen any of the series. 'Charles Paris—*Stanislas Braid*.'

She repeated the names, as if satisfied at having made a forgotten connection, but Charles reckoned it was also a way of entering the information into her mental filing system. He felt certain that, if they ever met again, she would greet him with 'Charles Paris, yes, of course. You were in that *Stanislas Braid* series, weren't you?'

It was a good skill to have, though, that kind of social memory, an essential skill for a busy hostess. Charles just wished he couldn't see the wheels turning quite so obviously as the machinery clicked into action.

Brian Tressider's manner may have been as studied as his wife's, but it seemed more spontaneous. He found a friendly word for everyone. Heather from the Dispatch Office had emerged to greet the boss, and coloured winsomely at some remark he threw at her.

Then he clapped an arm round Alan Hibbert's shoulder. 'Yes, don't tell me, Alan—this video's throwing all your scheduling to buggery.'

'Well, I'm afraid it is, B.T. We've got to get the regular Wednesday deliveries off and we can't wait around too long for—'

'Don't worry about it. You'll make up the time.'

'I can't see why we—'

'No, really, Alan, the video's important. I wouldn't have agreed to our doing it if I didn't think so. And if you lose half a day here in the warehouse, or if we lose a day's production even, it's not the end of the world.'

'Never thought I'd hear you talk like that, B.T.'

'Priorities change. Of course I want to maximise production, but keeping everyone's nose to the grindstone every second of the day may not be the best way of achieving that. Making everyone feel they *belong* to the company could be more effective in the long run. A contented workforce is an efficient workforce, Alan.'

The Warehouse Manager looked at his boss with a blatant scepticism that suggested their relationship went back a long way. 'Sounds like you've been reading another of those management books, Brian.'

The Managing Director let out a short laugh. 'Maybe I have.' He laughed again and turned to Griff Merricks. 'Tell me, how much more've you got to do here?'

'Couple more set-ups of Charles on the forklift. Just cutaways, really, for editing purposes.'

'How long do you reckon?'

'Half an hour top weight.'

'And how long to clear up?'

'Another half-hour?'

'And then you'll be out of Alan's hair?'

'No problem.'

'That's it then.' Brian Tressider turned back to his Warehouse Manager. 'Break all your staff now for early lunch—OK? Get them all back at two, and you'll be able to work through the afternoon with no interruptions.'

'All right.' Alan Hibbert went off to communicate this decision to his operators. They needed no second bidding to leave the warehouse, and had all vanished within seconds.

"Oh, and Griff..." the Managing Director went on, 'if you want to bring your boys up to the Executive dining room for a drink and some lunch when you're through, please feel invited.'

The was the best suggestion Charles Paris had heard all morning.

'That's very kind,' said the director. 'What, all of them?'

This question did not encompass as many as it would have done on a proper television OB. Union regulations do not apply for the making of non-broadcast material, so Griff's technical support comprised only a lighting cameraman and sound recordist.

'Well, all the ones who're wearing ties,' said Brian Tressider over his shoulder, as he took his wife's arm and led her towards the warehouse door.

Charles Paris caught the flicker of glee in Will Parton's eye.

But he was distracted from melancholy thoughts of his tielessness by a little scene which was taking place the other side of the warehouse. The girl Dayna stood by the door as Brian and Brenda Tressider approached, with Ken Colebourne and Robin Pritchard close behind them. When they were almost level with her, Dayna leant against the doorframe in a frankly voluptuous pose, and winked.

What was surprising about the gesture was its lack of subtlety. Almost as if she was parodying a vamp. It was the performance of someone either highly sophisticated or deeply naïve.

The Managing Director stopped in his stride for a moment, as if about to say something, but then thought better of it, and steered his wife out of the warehouse.

It had only lasted a second, and very few people had noticed the incident, but it did seem bizarre.

'Right,' said Griff Merricks, 'let's get these last few shots done quick as we can.'

'Sure,' said Will Parton. 'Then off to the Executive dining room for "a drink and some lunch", eh?' He grinned at Charles. 'That is—those of us who're wearing ties.'

Charles grimaced long-sufferingly back at him.

'Don't worry,' said Will in a voice heavy with mock-solicitude. 'I'm told the Rissoles and Spotted Dick in the staff canteen are out of this world.'

'Thank you very much.'

The writer shook his head sadly. 'Such a pity it's not licensed.'

IT'S REMARKABLE how quickly television people can work when they've got a proper incentive. The last few shots of Charles on the forklift truck were in the can within ten minutes and almost before he'd got out of his seat, the cables were all unplugged and coiled up, ready to be packed away. Within another half-minute, Will Parton, Griff Merricks, his cameraman and sound recordist had all disappeared in search of the Executive dining room.

Blatant discrimination, thought Charles. Meant to be living in an egalitarian society, and yet there's still this massive undercurrent of prejudice against people who don't wear ties. Huh.

He looked disconsolately round the empty warehouse. Through the windows of the ground-level office he could see Dayna and Heather involved in inaudible conversation.

A childish temptation gnawed at him. He moved back to the forklift truck and sat in it. Loaded shelves meant that he was out of sight of the office.

Really would be fun to make the lift work, wouldn't it? Raise and lower a pallet . . . ? Even see if he could pick one up perhaps . . . ?

He turned the key in the ignition. The engine started. He reached for the lifting controls.

But no. That was being stupid. Could easily cause a lot of damage. Press that 'Quick Release' button by mistake and you could send a whole pallet's load smashing down. Be your age, Charles Paris. ('Forty-eight, but play younger.')

Reluctantly, he switched the ignition off and got down from the truck.

Just as well, really. The girl Dayna was coming out of the office. If she saw what he was up to, she'd think he was out of his mind.

She didn't seem aware of his presence, but stood irresolute by the door. The room inside was empty. Heather must have retreated to her inner office.

Not wishing to draw attention to himself, Charles moved silently out of the warehouse, in search of the staff canteen.

Outside, he met Trevor who, with his habitual surliness, directed Charles Paris towards the delights of Rissoles and Spotted Dick.

FOUR

IN THE EVENT, he went for the Steak Pie and Jam Roly-Poly, impassively served from behind heated counters by hard-faced women in pale blue housecoats. The vegetables suffered from that sogginess endemic to British institutional food (and rather too much British restaurant food), but otherwise the meal tasted all right. And the prices were amazingly low. Delmoleen subsidised its employees' eating generously.

Any sneaking hope he had had that the canteen might be licensed was quickly dispelled, and, to his amazement, Charles found himself ordering a cup of tea with his lunch. It must have been the influence of the environment, and perhaps his costume, as his actor's instinct slotted him instantly into the role he was playing. Cup of tea, dollop of gelatinous custard...it made him feel as if he was back in one of those early sixties plays of social realism, something like Wesker's *Chips with Everything* ('The effeteness of Charles Paris's performance left me suspecting that the RAF would have turned him down on medical grounds'—*The Huddersfield Examiner*).

Still, he thought piously, good thing not to be drinking at lunchtime—although the righteous sensation of having satisfactorily finished his day's work deserved the reward of a quick one.

But no, it was good. Too few lunchtimes passed these days unassisted by drink. To have abstinence forced on him like this gave Charles the reassuring feeling that he wasn't an alcoholic. He could take it or leave it . . .

He would rather *take* it, obviously, but at least he wasn't chemically dependent . . .

Or probably wasn't.

He tried to put from his mind the image of Will Parton and Griff Merricks downing glasses of wine in the Executive dining room, and comforted himself with the promise of a large Bell's when he got back to his bedsitter in Hereford Road.

The canteen offered him the same measure of conviviality as it did of alcohol. Since he didn't know anyone there, he had hardly expected a hearty welcome and cheery hands waving him over to join tables, but he was surprised by the positive antipathy that exuded from the Delmoleen employees.

He was recognised as an outsider—probably the unfamiliar overalls didn't help—and as such he was suspect. While he looked around for a seat, he was first briefly scrutinised by the other diners and then pointedly ignored. Finally finding an empty table piled high with the detritus of earlier lunches, he sat down and ate his meal as quickly as possible.

HE HAD FINISHED inside ten minutes and it still wasn't one o'clock. He wandered outside the canteen. Knots of Delmoleen workers stood around smoking and chatting. Over on a bit of open ground an improvised game of football was under way. The only acknowledgement Charles's presence received was the odd deterrent stare.

He wondered at first if they could recognise him as an actor and were showing the traditional reaction to 'bleeding fairies'. But there was no way anyone could know his profession. Maybe they suspected him of being a management spy, a time and motion consultant. But that too was nonsense. No, he finally decided that he was incurring resentment simply because he was unfamiliar.

It wasn't a pleasant sensation, though. Charles felt tempted just to leave, catch a train, go home. Griff Merricks had said he only needed the few extra shots for editing and those were done.

On the other hand, in the pre-lunch confusion, Charles hadn't actually been granted an official release. And directors were notorious for changing their minds after a couple of drinks. Charles had been booked for the full day and his professionalism told him that he shouldn't leave until Griff Merricks gave him formal permission. The daily rate he was being paid was quite impressive, and Charles didn't want to screw up the chances of further work in this lucrative area by being absent when needed.

He contemplated finding a local pub to pass the next hour. But he hadn't seen any when he arrived at the station, and no doubt if there was one around, it would be just another outpost of the Delmoleen resentment of strangers.

Disconsolately, but vigorously, as if his movement had some purpose, Charles strode back towards the warehouse. He'd left his raincoat there, apart from anything else. And in his raincoat pocket was a potential lifesaver. Not, he reflected virtuously—if a little wistfully—a half-bottle of Bell's, but something much more wholesome—a copy of *Persuasion*. He did find rereading Jane Austen every few years wonderfully therapeutic.

As he entered the warehouse, the huge space was very still.

But it was not completely silent. From somewhere in the distant stacks Charles could hear the hum of an electric motor.

He moved towards the source of the sound.

It was in the aisle they had used for the filming. Where he had left his forklift truck, a pile of loose cartons, fallen from a shelf above, lay scattered on the ground. The truck itself had moved forward and was embedded into the pile of empty pallets which stood against the wall at the end of the aisle. Its engine still protested as it pressed against the slowly splintering wood.

Charles tried to work out what could have happened. If the ignition had been left switched on and the motor running, it was just possible, given the looseness of the gear lever, that one of the falling cartons could have knocked it and engaged the engine. Then the truck would have moved forward.

But that did assume that the motor had been left running.

And Charles knew he had switched the ignition off.

It was as he had this thought that he heard the other sound.

Lower than the mechanical hum of the forklift engine, and more human.

He moved forward, suddenly panicked.

Yes, through the slats of the pallets, slumped against the foot of the wall, he could see a human shape.

The moaning was ominously low and feeble.

Charles Paris leapt into the seat of the forklift and pulled the gear lever into reverse. The truck jerked back, dragging some of the pallets with it. Others toppled noisily to the ground.

Charles disengaged the gear and switched off the ignition.

Then he tugged at the heavy pile of pallets to clear them from the wall. His hands snagged on the rough wood. He was aware of splinters digging in, but felt no pain.

As he pulled back the last obstruction, the moaning was interrupted by a little gasp, almost a sigh of pain.

Charles looked down into the space he had cleared.

The limbs lay at odd angles, unnaturally compacted against the wall.

The shallow rasp of breathing could still just be heard from the crushed body, but blood trickled from the nose and mouth, indicating severe internal injury.

It was the girl, Dayna.

FIVE

HE LOOKED AROUND for help, but there was no one else in the warehouse. The girl was unconscious and looked ghastly, but vague recollections of the basic principles of first aid told Charles he shouldn't move an injured person. He'd just have to leave her and go for help.

He hurried up the aisle to the office at the back. There was no one in the outer room. He knocked on the interconnecting door and moved through into the inner office.

Brian Tressider and Heather looked up with surprise at his entrance, but without embarrassment. Nothing untoward had been going on, and indeed looking at the two of them—he wirily elegant, she frankly frumpy—it was an unlikely thought that anything might have been. She sat at her desk, an opened but untouched packet of sandwiches in front of her. He stood at the other side of the room.

The Managing Director cocked an interrogative eyebrow at Charles.

'There's been an accident. It's dreadful. In the warehouse. We need an ambulance.'

'What's happened? Who's been hurt?'

'Dayna.'

It seemed to Charles that, at the mention of the name, Heather searched Brian Tressider's face for some reaction. What she was expecting was hard to judge, but, whatever it was, the craggy face remained impassive.

'Get on to Security, Heather. And Personnel. They'll have a contact for her parents or next-of-kin. And find Alan Hibbert—quickly!'

'Yes, Brian.'

'I think you should call an ambulance first.'

Charles's suggestion was rewarded by a flash of anger from the Managing Director's grey eyes. 'Security will do that.' Brian Tressider didn't take kindly to being told how to run his company.

Just as she reached for the receiver, the telephone on Heather's desk rang. She picked it up. 'Oh, Mother, what is it *now*? Well, it *is* a bad moment. We've got an emergency on and . . .'

Brian indicated the door. 'Show me,' he commanded.

Charles Paris ushered him through the offices to the warehouse, and down the aisle to where the girl lay. Her breathing seemed even weaker. The pool of blood from mouth and nostrils was spreading ominously.

Brian Tressider showed no emotion. 'Did the pallets fall on her?'

'No, the forklift had somehow started and pushed them against her. I moved the truck back.'

The Managing Director gave a curt nod. 'Industrial accidents are buggers. Last thing you want in a place like this.' He looked back up the aisle to the scattered cartons. 'Those must've fallen and knocked the truck into gear.'

'Does that really seem likely?' asked Charles.

The flinty grey stare was turned on him. 'Well, I can't think what else happened, can you?'

'Just seems a coincidence. Anyway, somebody must've left the truck switched on.'

Brian Tressider shrugged. 'Happens all the time. Trucks keep having to be recharged when they shouldn't because some idiot's left them running. Dozy lot of buggers you get in a place like this.'

'But presumably you will investigate to find out who did leave it switched on?'

'Yes, we'll investigate.' His voice didn't express much confidence in the efficacy of the procedure. 'They'll all deny they were the last ones to touch it.'

'I think *I* was the last one to touch it. You know, in the filming.'

This prompted another sharp stare. 'Then I'd bloody well keep quiet about it, if I were you.'

'But I know I left it switched off.'

'Yes, I'm sure you did.' The scepticism in the tone was undisguised. Though he might not have used the expression 'bleeding fairies', Brian Tressider clearly shared the common prejudice against the theatrical profession.

He looked down at the injured girl and pursed his lips with annoyance. 'Why people can't just do what they're meant to do I'll never understand. Most industrial accidents occur because people are where they shouldn't be, or doing what they're not meant to be doing.'

'Well, what do you think she was doing behind the pallets?'

This got another shrug. Such speculation apparently held no interest for Brian Tressider.

They heard hurried footsteps and turned to see Alan Hibbert approaching. The Warehouse Manager took in the scene instantly.

'Shit,' he said softly.

'Yes. Shit,' Brian concurred. 'Is the nurse on her way from Surgery?'

A nod. 'And they've called an ambulance. She's still alive, isn't she?'

'At the moment. Not looking too good, though. Maybe we should put a blanket over her or something?'

The Warehouse Manager found a blanket and gently covered the still form. 'Silly girl. She was a right little mixer, B.T. Always poking her nose into things that weren't her business.'

Again the Managing Director didn't seem interested. The girl's behaviour was irrelevant. It was the inconvenience of the accident that seemed to preoccupy him. 'Have to do a full report, Alan, won't we...?'

The Warehouse Manager caught the slight interrogative inflection at the end of this. 'Sorry. No way round it. I must get on the blower to the Environmental Health Department straight away.'

'I'd hold fire till she's been moved to the hospital, if I were you,' said Brian Tressider.

Alan Hibbert looked at his boss in some surprise. Despite the softness of tone in which they had been spoken, the words had been not a suggestion, but an order.

THE WAREHOUSE STAFF who'd been involved in the video and the film crew who had made it were assem-

bled in Heather's back office an hour later for a de-
briefing from their Managing Director.

'Listen, we're all obviously very upset about what's
happened and I hope it's reinforced to the lot of you
working in this warehouse just how seriously the safety
regulations have to be followed. Now of course we're
going to have an internal investigation to find out exactly how the accident came about and to make sure
that this kind of thing can't happen again...isn't that
right, Alan?'

The Warehouse Manager nodded. He was completely solid with his boss. Both of them knew that an
investigation had to take place; neither of them wanted
that investigation to make any waves. All they did
want was for Delmoleen to return to business-as-usual
as soon as possible.

Already, Charles had noticed with some shock, the
site of the accident had been cleared up, sawdust scattered and swept away, disinfectant sprinkled. Along
the other aisles of the warehouse forklifts and stock-
pickers plied their trade, as the waiting lorries slowly
filled with Delmoleen products. Whatever kind of investigation did ensue, it wasn't going to have much to
go on from the forensic point of view.

'And it's quite likely,' Brian continued, 'that we
could be the subject of an external investigation too.
In fact, it's pretty well certain that the boys from the
Environmental Health Department will be along soon.

'I'm going to be in London and abroad for the next
few weeks, so I want to say to all of you now, that if
their inspectors do come round to talk to you, please
co-operate. Answer any questions they ask you, *but*—
and this is an important "but"—don't tell them more

than they ask. OK? No speculation, no comments about the poor kid's character—none of that stuff, all right?'

The assembled group nodded agreement. Ken Colebourne caught Robin Pritchard's eye and shook his head wryly.

'Isn't it possible,' Charles hazarded gently, 'that the police might also make some kind of investigation?'

A roomful of cold eyes focused on him.

'I wouldn't have thought that would be necessary,' said Brian Tressider. 'We are talking about an *accident* here.'

'Yes, but—'

The Managing Director's voice continued on a level note. He was not used to being interrupted. 'I would also have thought that a police investigation was something that you particularly would wish to avoid, Mr Paris—as the last person to leave the warehouse before the accident, *and* the last person to touch the forklift that caused it.'

'I'm fairly sure I wasn't the last person,' Charles persisted. 'I'm also positive that I switched the engine off when I left the truck.'

'I'd doubt that.' Now Trevor had joined in the argument. 'Did any of you see the way he was farting around on that forklift this morning—bloody hopeless? Hardly knew if it was in "forward" or "reverse". Can't expect a bloody actor to remember whether he's left it switched on or not.'

Without this aggression, Charles probably wouldn't have made a public accusation, but he was stung and spoke before he could stop himself. 'I know I switched it off,' he announced firmly, 'and I'm pretty sure that someone else switched it back on again. In fact, as I left the warehouse, I saw someone going in.'

Trevor sensed he was about to be named and came in quickly with his admission. 'All right, I was going in there, don't deny it. Left me fags. Just nipped in to get them.'

The operator blushed defiantly, judging that the pro-cover-up mood of the meeting would probably preclude further questions.

But he'd underestimated his Managing Director. Brian Tressider wanted the investigations to be concluded as quickly as possible, but he wasn't going to ignore this new information. 'Why didn't you mention this before, Trevor?'

The blush grew deeper. 'Like I said ... I just nipped in. I, er ... I ...'

He looked acutely uncomfortable, but salvation came from an unexpected source.

They all looked round as Heather spoke. 'That's right. I saw Trevor as he came into the warehouse. Then he came into my office for a chat. You remember, because my mother rang while you were here, didn't she, Trevor?'

There was an infinitesimal pause before the operator replied, 'Yes, Heather, that's right.'

Charles was convinced they were lying. 'So how long was Trevor with you?'

'Till about one, I suppose.'

Nearly all the time that Charles had been absent from the warehouse. He'd seen Trevor on the way out, gone to the canteen to eat his Steak Pie and Jam Roly-Poly, and apparently just missed Trevor on his return. What on earth had Heather and the forklift operator talked about for so long?

'Yes, it would have been one o'clock,' Heather went on, 'because that's when you came in, Brian. Trevor had just gone out *there*'—she indicated the door that led to the exterior—'when you came in from the warehouse, Brian.'

The Managing Director eyed the actor sardonically. 'Well, I think we seem to have sorted out Trevor's movements, anyway, Mr Paris.'

Charles wasn't satisfied. Nor could he provide a logical motive for Heather's rescue of Trevor. Perhaps it was done simply in the cause of company solidarity. Or maybe she nursed a secret passion for the operator. Heather must have been in her early fifties. She didn't look the sort of woman in whose life romance had featured much; so it was in theory possible that she might have a love object as unprepossessing as Trevor.

But whatever her motivation, Charles still didn't believe the alibi she had provided. 'Look, it still seems to me—'

He was interrupted by the ringing of the telephone on Heather's desk. She answered it. 'Yes. Oh, hello, Mrs Tressider. Yes, he's here. Brian.' The phone was handed across.

'Yes, darling? Mr and Mrs Richman? Oh, right. Well, say all the appropriate things. Yes, I'll come over and talk to them straight away. See you shortly.'

He handed the phone back to Heather, and sighed. 'Brenda's at the hospital, with the girl's parents. I'm afraid Dayna's just died.'

There were mixed reactions of shock and other sentiments appropriate to the announcement of a death.

Only Brian Tressider showed nothing.

And once again Charles was aware of Heather staring into her boss's face, looking for some reaction.

But what reaction she was expecting it was again impossible to tell.

SIX

NEEDLESS TO SAY, there wasn't a bar on the local service from Stenley Curton, nor were Charles Paris and Will Parton lucky enough to catch a properly equipped train from Bedford, so it was St Pancras before they could get a drink. And they needed it so much that they hardly noticed the unappealing surroundings of the station buffet. (Actually, to be truthful, environment never impinged that much on Charles's consciousness when he was drinking.)

They had hardly spoken on the journey, both shocked into silence and locked in their own thoughts. The first large Bell's went down without words, hardly touching the sides, but the second opened the floodgates.

'Do you know anything at all about the girl, Will?'

The writer shrugged. 'Not a lot. My in-depth study of the Delmoleen operation didn't get as far as the typing pool.'

'That's what she was—just a typist?'

'Come on, she was only about nineteen. She was hardly going to be Sales Manager, was she?'

'No. And you don't know anything else about her?'

'Just that she tended to be around a lot.'

'How do you mean?'

'Well, I've been over at Stenley Curton a good few times in the last months, and, whoever I had a meeting with, I always seemed to see Dayna Richman at some point. It was as if she was pushing herself forward all the time.'

'What does that suggest—that she had fallen madly in love with you?'

Will shook his head warily. 'No, Charles. It suggests that she had fallen madly in love with the idea of being on camera.'

'Ah. She saw appearing in a corporate video as the first step on the ladder to stardom? Hoping some major film director would spot her talent and catapult her to Hollywood?'

'Maybe something on those lines. Or maybe she just saw it as a way of getting noticed within the company. She was pretty ambitious, I gather. As you saw, liked attention. Hardly a shrinking violet.'

'Hardly. And presumably she worked in the Dispatch Office?'

'No, she didn't. I think she was in Personnel, some department like that. Though apparently she was always applying for other jobs. Really, Charles, I hardly know any more about her than you do.'

'You must at least know how she came to be in the video?'

Will Parton spread his hands wide. 'Think of what she looked like. You're doing a video to boost the in-house image of the company...so who do you show in the Dispatch Office—the frump or the vamp? Heather or Dayna?'

'See what you mean. So you reckon Dayna kept putting herself forward with just that outcome in mind?'

'I'd have thought so, Charles. And it worked, didn't it? She got the job.'

'Yes. And who would have given her that job—I mean, who actually said, "All right, Dayna, you do it"?'

'Be Ken Colebourne, I suppose. He's sort of in charge of the video from the Delmoleen end—he's the one I have to check everything with. So if he suggested Dayna to Griff ... well, Griff's hardly the kind of guy who's going to argue, is he?'

'No. Did you actually hear that exchange take place—I mean, hear the moment when Ken suggested Dayna should be in the video?'

Will screwed up his face as he tried to remember. 'Ye-es. Yes, I did. It was only a couple of weeks back. Griff just said fine. He was getting paid, he didn't care what was suggested.'

'No.'

Their glasses had unaccountably emptied themselves once again. Will went to the bar to remedy this defect. Charles looked thoughtful. His mind was buzzing with potential motivations. Taking the proffered refill from Will, he mused, 'Heather must've been pretty miffed.'

'Hm?'

'Heather—the one who runs the Dispatch Office. I mean, she doesn't look the sort of woman whose life has been full of excitements. For her to have been aced out of the video by some dolly bird who doesn't even work in the department must've been pretty galling.'

'Apparently not. No, according to Ken Colebourne, Heather was delighted.'

'Why?'

'Maybe hard for you, as an actor, to believe it, Charles, but there are people in this world who don't like showing off, people for whom the idea of being under public scrutiny is absolutely terrifying. It seems that Heather is one of those. Ken had asked her to be in the video, but the prospect appalled her. She kept begging him to find someone else, and when Dayna was suggested, Heather was over the moon.'

'Oh,' said Charles, disappointedly watching that particular conjecture crumble away. He moved on to another one. 'There had clearly been something going on between Dayna and Trevor, hadn't there?'

The writer lifted his shoulders dismissively. 'Could've been.'

'Oh, come on, Will. It was obvious. Did you see the way he reacted when she arrived? Up until that moment, he'd been all keen to do more in the video, then suddenly he goes cold on the whole idea. They must've been having an affair, or just've broken off an affair or...'

'Charles,' said Will with deliberately infuriating condescension, 'there are other motivations in life apart from sex.'

'Maybe, but—'

'Just because you're obsessed with the subject, and just because, as a dirty old man, you can't look at a pretty young girl without immediately wondering who's bonking her, it doesn't mean that everyone is the same.' He affected the drawl of intellectual pretension. '*As a writer*, of course, I have a much deeper understanding of the multifarious nature of human motivations.'

Will had given too good a cue to the counter-attack for Charles to ignore it. 'And, *as a writer*, do tell me— what are you going to be working on next? Can it be that you're finally about to start on the new play we've all heard so much about?'

The barb found its target. Will Parton coloured. 'No. That'll have to wait. I've still got quite a lot to do on the Delmoleen front, as it happens.'

'What, more out at Stenley Curton?'

'Uhuh. Few more bits showing what a united company it is. Bijou scenettes in some of the offices, shots of the actual manufacturing process, staff relaxing in the canteen, high jinks in the firm's social club, all that. And then, if I play my cards right, I might secure *Parton Parcel* the contract for the Delmoleen sales conference in Brighton at the end of September.'

'I see. This one could run and run.'

'With a bit of luck, yes.'

'Well, if any of those bijou scenettes might involve a forklift truck operator capable of speech, do let me know.'

'Now taking bookings, are you, Charles?'

'Well, I do actually have a few free days... Just the odd one or two... Well, any time really... Any date you care to mention, between now and my death... And, if it's a really good part, I won't let a little thing like that stop me.'

'So I just get in touch with your agent, do I?'

'Don't you dare! Keep Maurice out of this. No, anything corporate, do it direct.'

'OK.' Will dropped the bantering tone. 'Actually, there could be a bit in the canteen sequence. Need someone to talk there.'

'I'll happily expatiate on the virtues of the Jam Roly-Poly for you.'

'May well take you up on that. I'll let you know.'

'I've heard that line before somewhere...can't think where. Still, it would be great if there is anything.' Charles grimaced thoughtfully. 'No, I'd really like to get back to Stenley Curton.'

'What, for—?' Will looked at his friend despairingly. 'Oh, Charles, *no*.'

Charles Paris looked the picture of aggrieved innocence. 'What are you on about?'

'This is like on the *Stanislas Braid* series, isn't it? You see this as the start of an investigation. You just don't believe in the philosophical concept of an *accident*. You think that girl Dayna Richman was murdered, don't you?'

'Yes, I do,' said Charles.

Will Parton groaned. Charles Paris went to refill their glasses.

'FRANCES, IT'S ME.'

'Ah,' said his wife's voice from the other end of the phone.

'Charles.'

'Yes, Charles, I do know who you mean. My "Ah" was not an "Ah" of incomprehension, but an "Ah" of "Ah. That is my husband on the phone."'

'Is that a good sort of "Ah"?' he asked hopefully.

'I wouldn't plan your retirement on it.'

'Ah.' There was a silence. 'I just rang because—'

'You just rang because I had almost reached a state of equanimity about our marriage.'

'What?'

'You have an uncanny sense of timing, Charles.'

'Oh?' To an actor that had to be a compliment.

'Every time I reconcile myself to the fact that we really are finished, and that I won't ever hear from you again, and it's just as well, and now thank God I can get on with the rest of my life...you ring up.'

'Ah.'

'Always at exactly that precise moment.'

He let out a little, tentative laugh. 'Well, that must say something, mustn't it?'

'Huh. I don't think you'd like it if I spelled out what it *does* say, Charles.'

'No, no, fine. Well, leave that as read,' he said hastily.

'So...to what do I owe the pleasure of this call? You've missed my birthday, it's not Christmas yet, so what is it—some mutual form, some documentary relic left over from the days of our marriage, that needs countersigning?'

'No, Frances. No, it's just, er...I wanted to talk to you.'

'Why suddenly now? What is so different about to-day, as opposed to any other day in the last four months when you could have wanted to talk to me?'

'Oh, surely it's not as long as—'

'Four months,' she said implacably.

'Well, I...' He opted for vulnerability. 'Well, I've been feeling a bit low and...'

It was a bad choice. 'Everyone feels low from time to time, Charles.'

'Yes...'

'It's just that some of us don't go on about it all the time.'

'No, of course. I just—'

'Charles, why are you ringing?'

'Well, it was kind of to make contact and—'

'You've made contact. If you have anything else to say, say it. I've got someone here.'

He was shocked by how much her words hurt. Recovering himself, he said, 'I was wondering if we could get together...'

'What for?' she demanded brusquely.

'Well, for a...you know, for a drink...for a meal...just to see each other...'

'Hm.'

'I mean, that's what other married couples do, isn't it?'

'I wouldn't use the "other married couples" line with me, Charles, if I were you. It doesn't go down very well.'

'No. Well...I... As I say, just be nice to see you.'

All this got was another 'Hm'.

'As I say, just for a drink or...'

'I'd rather it wasn't just for a drink, Charles.'

'What do you mean?'

'I've served my time hanging round grotty pubs and wine bars, waiting for you to turn up...'

'I wouldn't be late. I'd—'

'No, if you want to see me, you invite me somewhere nice.'

'Nice?'

'Yes. You think of something nice, that I—not *you*—but *I* would like to do, and when you've thought of it, you ring me up and invite me to it.'

'Ah.'

'And then, if I like the sound of it, and if I happen to be free on the relevant date... then I'll accept the invitation.'

'Right. Erm, but, Frances—'

'Bye, Charles.'

He stayed by the pay phone on the Hereford Road landing after he had put the receiver down, still smarting. It was ridiculous to feel like this. Surely he'd long since abrogated any right to feel jealous of Frances.

Why should he imagine that she would always be on her own when he called? Given the amount he was contributing to it, he could hardly criticise her for the way she chose to conduct her own social life.

And, anyway, 'someone here' could mean anything. A fellow-schoolmistress. Any one of her many women friends. An elderly neighbour. A Jehovah's Witness.

He was being stupid and he knew it.

But he was still surprised at how much it hurt.

IN AN ATTEMPT to shift his thoughts, he dialled another number.

'Maurice Skellern Artistes.'

'Maurice—it's Charles.'

'Oh yes, how're things? Got any work?'

Charles found himself blushing as he replied, 'No. Surely that's a question an actor should ask his agent rather than the other way round?'

'Oh, I don't know, Charles. Hear so many cases these days of clients getting work behind their agents' backs and not even telling them.'

'Ah. Do you?' Charles laughed uneasily. 'So, anyway, you heard of anything coming up?'

The reply was so familiar he could have joined in. 'Not a dicky bird, Charles. Things are very quiet at the moment, very quiet.'

'Hm.'

'Not a good time right now...you know, with the summer coming up.'

'Sure, and then it'll be the autumn coming up, won't it, Maurice? And that won't help.'

'You're right there, Charles. And then we'll be on to the winter, and nobody makes any decisions when there's Christmas just round the corner, do they?'

'No. So we'll just have to wait till the spring, won't we?'

'Yes...' There was a pause. 'Mind you, that's never a lot better either, is it?'

As he put the phone down, Charles wondered why on earth he had imagined that a call to his agent might possibly cheer him up. As always, it just left him more depressed than ever.

And on this occasion—infuriatingly—because of the work he'd been doing for Delmoleen, it also left him feeling slightly guilty.

SEVEN

WITHIN A couple of weeks Charles Paris once again found himself doing work his agent didn't know about. Will had managed to swing it that one of the 'bijou scenettes' in the canteen did involve a forklift operator capable of speech, so once again Charles was to don the pristine Delmoleen overalls and give his impression of Trevor.

It was a bit like being a stuntman, he reflected, though whereas stuntmen did physical tricks for people who could act, he was doing acting tricks for someone who could manage the physical stuff with no assistance.

This time he wasn't the only actor involved. When he met Will Parton at St Pancras, the writer introduced a tall figure by his side. 'Charles Paris—this is Seb Ormond.'

It transpired on the train journey that Seb Ormond was one of those actors who specialised in corporate work. Indeed, it was a long time since he had set foot on a stage or performed in a film or television production that was seen by the general public. But his conversation left no doubt that he made a very good living from his 'in-house' career.

To Charles it was a constant source of amazement how many specialties there were within his profession, and the broad range of work that being an actor could encompass. He often suspected that the ones who specialised were the shrewd ones. As in any other area of entrepreneurial life, what such actors had to do was to carve out little niches for themselves, maintain the standards of their work, build up goodwill and, hopefully, make themselves indispensable. Charles knew actors who did that in commercial voice-overs, Victorian music hall, cruise ships entertainment and many other unlikely areas.

Sometimes he regretted that he had never carved out such a niche for himself, but always came back to the view that doing the same thing all the time must get very boring. Doing nothing all the time—which was the pattern that his life seemed to be following these days—was also boring, but at least he could dream of potential employment in every branch of show business (even though so few jobs in any branch actually materialised).

Seb Ormond was one of the names on the *Parton Parcel* letterhead. He wasn't actually a partner, but had an agreement with the company whereby, when Will needed an impressively-suited figure for a business meeting, Seb would turn up. For a substantial fee. *Gravitas* didn't come cheap.

He was also, of course, available for ordinary work as a corporate actor. Which was how he had been booked for that day at Stenley Curton. Again for a substantial fee. Considerably more than Charles Paris was being paid.

Seb Ormond was dressed in a dark suit with a discreet stripe, a shirt with an even more discreet stripe, and a tie the discretion of whose stripe would have qualified it for the Diplomatic Service. On the station platform he melted into the crowd—just another executive commuter. Only the fact that he was catching a morning train *out* of St Pancras rather than arriving on one coming *in* might have raised any suspicion about his identity.

'Seb's Management today,' Will Parton explained unnecessarily. 'Ken Colebourne's decided that he wants to demonstrate Delmoleen's egalitarianism, so we're going to have an executive mucking in with the riff-raff in the canteen.'

'And none of the real exeuctives'd do it?' asked Charles.

'Good heavens, no. None of them'd be seen dead in the canteen. Anyway, this executive has to *talk*.'

'Aren't the Delmoleen employees who see this video going to think it odd that they don't recognise any of the people in it?'

'Not that odd. It's quite a big company. Stenley Curton's not the only site. Anyway, I sometimes wonder whether anyone ever will see the video.'

'Why?'

'Well, Ken Colebourne seems pretty ambivalent about it—don't know that he ever thought it was that great an idea. Reading between the lines, I reckon it's something Brian Tressider foisted on to him and now Brian's abroad, not breathing down his neck all the time, Ken's lost interest. He's of the old school..."never had videos in our time and it didn't do us any harm..."you know the sort.'

Charles nodded. 'But they're not going to cancel the production?'

'Oh no, contract with *Parton Parcel*'s all sewn up. The thing'll get *made*—they're committed to that. Just may never get *shown*.'

'Ah.'

'Still, that hardly matters to any of us, does it?'

They all agreed that, so long as they got paid, it couldn't have mattered less.

Seb Ormond was happy to share his experience of corporate work with Charles—indeed, it would have been hard to prevent him from doing so.

'Thing you've got to do is get the clothes right, Charles. Go up for an interview in the wrong kit and you may as well forget it.'

'Yes, I'd heard that.'

'So you've got to be sure you've been properly briefed. I went up for one where they were looking for an Estate Manager, and my bloody agent told me it was an Estate Agent. As you can imagine—total disaster!'

'Do you do most of this stuff through your agent?' asked Charles, once again feeling rather guilty.

'No, I fix the bulk of it myself, but because I do so much, the agent does get enquiries.'

Charles felt marginally less guilty.

'So you've got to sort out the basic wardrobe.' Seb Ormond looked across at Charles who, although fairly confident he would once again be given the overalls, had dressed in his 'Trevor' costume. 'Of course, I don't do many blue collar roles...'

'No. Well, obviously...' And it was obvious. Seb Ormond's patrician feathers and greying hair had 'Management' stamped all over them.

'So the basic wardrobe I have is what I think of as the Managing Director's suit, the Sales Manager's suit, the Bank Manager's suit, and the Ad Agency suit.'

'And these are all different?'

'You better believe it, Charles.'

'Can I ask which suit you're wearing today... ?'

'Today's Sales Manager.'

'Oh. Right.'

'Back in the old days I got most of my basic wardrobe off tellies I did.'

'What, buying them at the end of the series?'

Seb Ormond nodded. The practice they referred to was common among actors. At the beginning of a television series, running characters would be taken shopping by the Wardrobe Department to kit out the part they were playing, and at the end there was an arrangement whereby these clothes, frequently much more costly than the actor could have run to in normal circumstances, were sold to him at a very reduced rate.

Charles could identify the productions which had dressed a lot of his actor friends, particularly in really expensive items like leather jackets. And of course actresses playing characters with designer tastes had a field day.

Charles himself had done less well out of this system than others in his profession. This was partly because he rarely got running parts and, when he did, they tended not to be people who dressed in his style. Recent forays into television would have netted him the blazer and trousers of a golf club barman or the uniform of a 1930s police sergeant, neither of which he felt was quite 'Charles Paris'.

'*Now*, of course,' Seb went on, 'I buy my own clothes.' He responded to Charles's quizzical look. 'Well, it is quite a while since I did ordinary telly. And

fashions do change, you know. Can't turn up as an
MD in a suit whose cut's five years out of date, can
you?'

'Ah, no,' agreed Charles Paris, whose one suit had
recently celebrated its Silver Jubilee. He avoided the
sardonic eye of Will Parton who had seen the garment in question.

What Seb Ormond was saying gave Charles a
strange sense of *déjà vu*. It reminded him of old ac-
tor-laddies he had heard reminiscing about repertory
theatre in the twenties and thirties. 'In those days, of
course,' they would ramble on, 'you had to have your
own basic costumes. Dinner suit was essential, and a
grey pinstripe, and tweeds as well. Otherwise you
didn't get the job. No Wardrobe Department to provide that sort of stuff in those days. And, my God, the
hours you'd work! Be playing one show at night, re-
hearsing the next following morning, learning lines for
a third...'

He was brought back to the present by the unsur-
prising fact that Seb Ormond was still talking. 'Some
characters you get asked to do, of course, need a touch
of fine tuning on the costume front. I mean, easy
enough to choose the right suit, but shirt and tie may
need a bit of thought. I did a GP last week.'

'Oh, really?'

'Basic Bank Manager's suit, shirt with slightly
frayed collar and hospital tie that was just a little bit
greasy. Worked a treat. Shall I tell you how well it
worked?'

'Go on,' Charles fed obligingly.

'The Medical Advisor on the film, who really was a
GP, turned up in the identical costume.'

'I say. Well done.'

'Wasn't bad, though I say it myself.' Seb Ormond smiled with modest self-congratulation. 'Buggers, medical ones, though.'

'Oh?'

'Well, a good few of them are for drug companies. You have to remember these great long names of chemical formulas and what-have-you. Real killers, some of those. Investment and insurance aren't much fun, either—lot of that stuff reads like absolute garbage. Just have to learn it by rote, as you would a foreign language, and hope to God you've got the pronunciation right. I must say, learning Beckett or Stoppard's a doddle compared to some of the scripts you get given on the corporates.'

'Haven't given you anything difficult today,' said Will Parton smugly.

'Oh no, today's a real treat from the script point of view. Do it standing on my head. Nice words, Will.'

The writer, whose great play remained resolutely unwritten, preened himself at this compliment on his Delmoleen dialogue.

Seb Ormond evidently enjoyed the centre stage position and held on to it. 'Actually, funny thing on that medical video the other week. As I say, I was meant to be a GP and it was actually shot in a real GP's surgery. The way it goes...I have a patient in there, I have to go to a filing cabinet, get out his records and say, "Well, I'm sorry, Mr Whatever, the current treatment doesn't seem to be working. What I recommend..." etc. Get halfway through it, look down at the file and see the notes have DIED printed across them in large letters. Now I never corpse, but I'm afraid that just got to me—pissing myself with laughter I was.

'OK, I sober up, go for Take Two—pick up another file—exactly the same thing. DIED it says. I break up again. Turns out the entire cabinet was full of files of dead people. Shouldn't have live ones, you see—breach of medical confidentiality.'

'Ah,' said Charles. 'Right.'

'You done a lot of corporate stuff, have you?' Seb Ormond asked magnanimously, maybe opening up the conversation for Charles to bring in a few anecdotes of his own.

'No. Lot of theatre, of course.'

'Oh, *that*,' said Seb Ormond dismissively.

THE CAMERA caused quite a stir in the canteen. The *Parton Parcel* crew had started work early, catching the last of the breakfast and the first of the tea-break trade, but nonetheless their presence prompted a lot of jockeying for position at adjacent tables by staff who wanted to be in shot.

Charles was yet again amazed at the potency of television and its ability to cloud the judgement. The chance of appearing on a screen, in whatever context, could turn the heads of people who in every other respect seemed to be completely sane. What else could explain the recurrent phenomenon of ordinary members of the public actually *volunteering* for the ritual humiliation of television game shows?

This thought also prompted Charles to wonder how much taking part in the Delmoleen video had meant to the late Dayna Richman; and how much she would have been prepared to do to ensure that she did get into it.

The morning's filming was straightforward, and the atmosphere more relaxed than it had been in the warehouse. Work on the video was not disrupting production in any way, and the impassive women dispensing tea and coffee from their urns showed no signs of resentment (or of anything else, come to that). No officious Canteen Manager was on hand to monitor the shooting, and Ken Colebourne, who was vaguely keeping an eye on things, seemed to be in a genial mood.

Charles and Seb Ormond delivered their lines with professional exactness, and Griff Merricks, exuding his customary negative charisma, was easily satisfied with what they did. The whole shoot was wrapped by noon, just as the canteen started to fill with early lunchers.

Will Parton looked at his watch. 'Executive dining room then, is it, Ken?'

'Well, yes, sure.'

The writer grinned smugly across at his friend. 'Oh dear, not improperly dressed again, are we, Charles?'

'Surely I'll be all right? If I keep the overalls on. These overalls are a darned sight smarter than any suit I possess.'

'That, Charles, is a comment on your suits rather than on the overalls.'

'Ha, bloody ha, Will.' Charles appealed to the Marketing Director. 'It doesn't really matter whether I'm in a suit or not for the Executive dining room, does it?'

But he had underestimated the hieratic structure of a company like Delmoleen. Ken Colebourne grimaced awkwardly. 'I'm afraid it isn't really possible, Charles. I mean, obviously, nothing personal, but there might be other people having lunch there who thought you were actually on the workforce and getting some kind of extra privilege. Wouldn't look good.'

'Oh,' said Charles, crestfallen.

Will gave him a patronising pat on the arm. 'Never mind. Who's the lucky boy? I notice the canteen's got Irish Stew on the menu today.'

'Thanks a bundle.'

Ken Colebourne didn't know how seriously to take this banter, but recognised a potential social problem. 'Erm, sorry. It's not that I want to appear inhospitable or anything...'

'Doesn't matter. Don't worry about it.'

But the Marketing Director did worry about it. This challenge to his diplomatic skills had taken on a disproportionate importance for him. He coloured and looked awkward. 'I really am sorry, Charles.'

'Don't be. It's no problem.'

'No, but I... Look...' A solution presented itself. 'Tell you what, rest of you go off to the Executive dining room—I'll stay here and have lunch with Charles.'

'You don't have to. I'm fine.'

But, having satisfactorily negotiated his way out of the awkwardness, Ken Colebourne would brook no opposition to his plans. He went to one of the internal phones to ensure the video party's welcome in the

Executive dining room, and then joined Charles in the queue for canteen lunch.

Resisting the seductions of the Irish Stew, Charles opted for Steak and Kidney Pie. To follow, he once again went for the Jam Roly-Poly, a delicacy that wasn't often on offer in the pubs and restaurants he frequented. As his portion—a whorl of sponge veined with vermilion jam—was dolloped into a bowl, he was forcibly reminded of the dish's schoolboy nickname, 'Dead Man's Leg'.

'As a matter of fact,' said Ken Colebourne when they had found a free formica-topped table and embarked on their first course, 'I find it quite a relief to eat in here sometimes. You can only take so much of posh, I reckon.'

Though this was undoubtedly said in part to alleviate the pain of Charles's exclusion from executive dining, the Marketing Director did sound as if he meant what he said.

'So you come in here often, do you?'

'Every now and then.'

'Oh, you should have been in the video—an authentic member of Management who actually eats in here. Could have done Seb Ormond out of a job.'

Ken Colebourne recoiled at the idea. 'No, thank you. Do anything rather than stand up and talk more than I have to. Sales conference is nearly four months away and already I wake up nights sweating about the presentation I got to do them. I know it's part of modern management—communicating, packaging yourself, packaging your ideas—but I must say I wouldn't mind winding the clock back a few years on all that stuff. I mean, the Sales Manager I used to work for in the sixties, only communication technique he used was telling us all to get our bloody fingers out. And it worked.'

'So you started as a salesman, did you?'

'Well, no, got promoted to salesman. Out of school I was a runner in the warehouse.'

'On the forklifts?'

'Didn't have many of those when I started. Used trolleys. Scurried back and forth along the stacks, picking up the stock by hand, then loading it on to the lorries.'

'Was it fun?'

'Well, the work was bloody boring, but then most work is, isn't it? Good bunch of lads, though, we had some laughs. Spent all our spare time playing football—that's all we thought about, really. That and the birds, of course.'

'You sound as if you'd like to be back there.'

'Well...' The Marketing Director sighed. 'Lot of ways things were much simpler then. Minute you walked out of the building you stopped thinking about work—didn't think about it much while you was doing it, come to that.'

'Whereas now...'

'Yeah. Whereas now...' The simple repetition adequately expressed his change of circumstances.

'Responsibilities...' Charles prompted.

'You can say that again. And new management techniques, and training programmes, and brainstorming sessions, and management consultants, and bloody videos and...'

'It sometimes seems to me,' Charles suggested cautiously, 'that there's a kind of connection between how badly business is going and the amount of training that gets done.'

'Too right. These days, when the product isn't selling, they don't put more effort into selling it, just more effort into training people how to sell it.'

'And are Delmoleen products not selling?'

Ken Colebourne shrugged. 'It's tough everywhere. Country's on the edge of recession, if it hasn't actually already tipped over. No, it's always been tough—just the way people try to deal with the problem changes.'

His tone left little doubt that he preferred the old solutions to those currently being offered.

'And I don't care much for the new style of management that's come in,' he continued. 'Back in the old days you knew people, you had friends, you thrashed things out over a few beers. Now it's all so impersonal... Sit there at endless meetings sipping Perrier, listening to all this jargon and bullshit... I feel like a fish out of water most of the time. Not really my scene, modern management.'

'Still, you've done all right,' said Charles reassuringly. 'Warehouse runner to Marketing Director—that's a pretty good progression, isn't it?'

'Oh yeah,' Ken Colebourne agreed wearily. 'Always the way in business—only way up is to move away from what you're good at. I've been in my current job seven years. That's a long time for this kind of work. Don't know how much longer I'll keep it.'

'Are you under threat then?'

'Everyone's under threat these days. Marketing's the sort of department that can easily get clobbered. You know, management changes...'

'Mm.' Charles had a sudden thought. 'Did Brian Tressider come up the same way as you?'

'What makes you ask that?'

'I don't know. The way you and he behave together . . . sort of suggests you go back a long way.'

'Well, you're right. We were at school together, here in Stenley Curton. Both joined Delmoleen on the same day. Alan Hibbert came in round that time too. Of course, Brian was the one who was always going on to great things.'

'You've done all right yourself.' Charles repeated the reassurance.

'Yes. He looks after his own, Brian.'

There were volumes of subtext in this sentence. Charles read it in Ken Colebourne's basic insecurity, his distrust of his own abilities, his fear that he had risen through the ranks of Delmoleen on the coat-tails of his more successful friend.

'Doesn't strike me as the kind of person who'd let sentiment stand in his way if he didn't think someone was pulling their weight.'

'No. No, I suppose not.' But Ken Colebourne didn't sound as if he believed it, more as if he was trying to convince himself.

'Unusual these days, isn't it, for a company to have many in management like you two, who've come up through the ranks . . . ?'

'Very unusual. And getting more unusual by the day. The business school graduates are taking over everywhere.' He grimaced his opinion of this development. 'No, Delmoleen is unusual. Lot of people still here I've known virtually since I started.'

'What about Trevor?' Charles asked casually. 'He been here long?'

For the first time in their conversation, Ken Colebourne looked guarded. 'Quite a while. Since he left school.'

'Just like you.'

'Yes. Mind you, he's twenty years younger than me.'

'Mm.' Charles spread the congealing duvet of custard over his Dead Man's Leg. 'Was there something between him and that girl Dayna?'

A shutter of caution came down over Ken Colebourne's eyes. 'I don't know what you're talking about.'

'An affair.'

'An affair between Dayna and *Trevor*?' He seemed genuinely astonished by the idea. 'But there was no way that . . .'

He thought better of finishing the sentence.

'There was something going on,' Charles persisted. 'Trevor behaved very strangely when Dayna came into the warehouse that morning . . . you know, the day she died.'

The shutter stayed down. 'I didn't notice anything odd.'

'Well, it was odd, you take my word for it.'

The Marketing Director became engrossed in his Lemon Meringue Pie. 'Big place like this, a lot of relationships start up, break up . . . Goes on all the time. And then a lot of totally unfounded rumours of relationships start up and get gossiped about. I make a point of not listening to any of it, and you'd do well to do the same.'

'But surely you—'

'It's not actually part of my job to know precisely who's bonking who at any given moment.'

'No, obviously it's not. I'm just asking you if you happen to know whether Trevor and Dayna had ever gone around together.'

Ken Colebourne concentrated on severing the end from his wedge of Lemon Meringue Pie.

'I've no idea,' he said.

But Charles Paris was left in no doubt that the Marketing Director was lying.

EIGHT

KEN COLEBOURNE downed the last of his Lemon Meringue Pie quickly, suddenly remembering someone he had to see about some artwork. He rattled out another quick apology about the Executive dining room, made a perfunctory goodbye, and was gone.

Thereby raising Charles Paris's suspicions even more.

Why should his question have proved such a source of embarrassment? Had Charles been asking about some connection between Dayna and the Marketing Director himself, then the reaction might have been justified.

If he really had nothing to hide, Ken Colebourne could have answered a simple 'Yes' or 'No'—or even a bluff 'Mind your own bloody business' to the enquiry about Dayna and Trevor's relationship. By behaving as he did, he had raised the spectre of his own involvement with one or both of them.

It was a matter on which Charles would have to find out more.

Because the passage of time did not dilute his conviction that Dayna Richman had been murdered.

Charles knew he had left the forklift's ignition switched off. Sometimes, he was aware, especially when he had been drinking, recollections of his actions were hazy, but on that occasion he hadn't touched a drop all morning (not even the quick pre-teeth-cleaning snort of Bell's which was becoming a regrettable habit these days). He had even been particularly abstemious the night before, not wishing to screw up his first foray into a new and potentially lucrative area of work. No, he'd left the ignition switched off all right.

So, at the very least, somebody had entered the deserted warehouse to switch it on again. And there would have been no point in doing that, unless the somebody in question had wanted to use the truck. The forklift certainly hadn't been used to shift any stock, but it had been used to crush the girl.

What had Dayna been doing there, anyway? Why on earth should a girl dressed up to look her best on camera go scrabbling behind a pile of dirty pallets?

Charles decided that, while he was on Delmoleen premises, he should try to have a little look round the warehouse, see if there was anything hidden between the pallets and the wall that Dayna might have been searching for.

Though anything that had been there would probably have been tidied up in the course of the investigations into her death.

These investigations, Charles had gathered that morning from Ken Colebourne, had now been completed. The in-house enquiry had come up with recommendations that Delmoleen staff restrict their movements to the work areas where they had business to be—which was tantamount to saying that, if Dayna hadn't been where she shouldn't have been, the accident wouldn't have happened. Or, in other words, that her death had been her own fault.

There had also been an investigation from the Environmental Health Department, whose finding had been quoted at the girl's inquest. They echoed the strictures of the in-house enquiry, and made other specific safety recommendations for application in the warehouse.

The police had not been involved, but then, in a case of industrial accident, why should they be?

Charles wondered if the situation would have been different had the girl been killed outright. If he had discovered a corpse rather than a fatally injured person, maybe the police would have been summoned.

But somehow he doubted it. The whole business gave off a smell of cover-up. Within the Delmoleen site, the company seemed to do its own policing. The 'accident' having happened, it had been dealt with quickly and efficiently, in a way that caused minimum publicity and minimum disruption to company business. If anyone other than Charles Paris had had a suspicion of murder, he got the feeling they would have suppressed it—or perhaps been persuaded to suppress it—in the cause of Delmoleen.

Or was he getting paranoid?

'THAT ONE'S THE ACTOR, is it?' he heard a loud, crackly voice say as he was leaving the canteen.

Half-turning to the source of the noise, he saw an elderly woman in a fur-collared overcoat sitting at a table with Heather from the Dispatch Office. The elderly woman's lips moved continuously, softly smacking against each other, as if she was talking all the time.

If the similarity in the set of the two women's eyes had not informed him, then Heather's reaction would have given away the fact that the older woman was her mother. There is a distinctive, atavistic, excruciating form of embarrassment that only parents can engender, and evidence of it glowed on Heather's cheeks. 'There's no need to be so loud. He'll hear you,' she hissed.

Her mother was not a whit perturbed. Seeing Charles looking in their direction, she immediately addressed him. 'Hello. My daughter says you're in this film they're making.'

He admitted that he was. Heather blushed even deeper as her mother said, 'Would you like to sit down with us? There's still tea in the pot.'

He was unsure whether the pain in Heather's eyes would be aggravated more by his acceptance or by his refusal, but, seeing a possible opening for further investigation, he drifted across to join them.

'Get the gentleman a cup.'

Heather seemed relieved to have somewhere to take her blushes and moved obediently across to the beverage counter.

'My name's Charles Paris.' He proferred his hand.

The old woman shook it. Hers was dry and scaly. 'Mrs Routledge. I'm Heather's mother.'

'I thought you must be.'

'She's a good girl, my daughter. Every Wednesday she gives me lunch here in the canteen. Gets me out of the house, you know, gives me a chance to see people a bit.'

'Yes.'

Heather returned wordlessly and put a Pyrex cup and saucer down in front of Charles. Mrs. Routledge, as was appropriate, acted as 'Mother' and poured in milk and tea. She had the sugar-shaker poised before he managed to stop her.

'I was just telling Mr Paris what a good daughter you are to me, Heather.'

The younger woman almost imperceptibly cringed. Mrs Routledge was using that distinctive kind of parental commendation which is infinitely more diminishing than insults. 'I'm such a lucky old lady to have a daughter who looks after me so well. We live together, you know...'

Charles just managed to interpose an 'Ah' into this stream of consciousness.

'Always have done. I encouraged Heather to get away when she was younger, but she never seemed to have the will really, did you, love?' It was clear that most of Mrs Routledge's questions were rhetorical, as she steamrollered on, 'So it's just the two of us. Heather's father died...ooh, how many years ago is it now, Heather?' But again she supplied her own answer. 'Twenty-seven, it is. Twenty-seven years ago. And since then there's just been the two of us. You're an actor, you say?'

Assuming that, despite this sudden change of direction, Mrs Routledge's conversational method would not alter, Charles said nothing.

His tactics were proved to be correct. 'Yes, Heather said you were. And you've been here working on this film they're making all about Delmoleen, isn't that right? I thought so. You know, they wanted Heather to be in the film. Yes, they did. They wanted to film her in her office. She didn't have to say anything, just sit there and be filmed. But she didn't want to. I said she was being silly. I said, there's no harm in just sitting there, the camera won't bite you, it's silly to be so shy. I've always said she should push herself forward a bit more. But you wouldn't do it, would you, Heather?'

In the course of this monologue, Charles caught its subject's eye. Beneath Heather's embarrassment gleamed an undercurrent of sheer blind anger. He gave her a half-smile; she responded with a wry tightening of her lips.

Now he looked closely at her, he saw that Heather Routledge was not an unattractive woman. The grey eyes were flecked with blue, and her skin had a tactile sheen. It was only the anonymous dowdiness of her clothes and awkwardness of her stance that created the image of ugliness. Illuminated by a little self-confidence, she would actually have been rather attractive.

'Still, there's no way I'm criticising my daughter. Oh no, I'm very lucky, and I'm not one of those old ladies who doesn't appreciate her good fortune. I'm extremely grateful for everything my daughter does for me. Do you know, Mr Paris, except for Wednesdays when she invites me in here, Heather rings me from work every single lunchtime.'

He managed to slip in an appreciative nod at this point.

'Yes, I'm very lucky. Every lunchtime. And she talks for a long time.'

Given Mrs Routledge's taste for monologue, this sounded unlikely, but neither of them questioned it.

Years of experience had dissuaded Heather from taking issue with anything her mother said, and Charles
found that he was subsiding into the same mesmer-
ised acceptance.

'Every lunchtime,' Mrs Routledge repeated. Then,
confident of the total subjugation of her audience, she
allowed herself a slurp of tea. 'Ooh, this is getting very
stewed. Go and get us some more hot water, Heather
love.'

Her daughter, an obedient automaton, went back to
the beverage counter and tried to attract the attention
of one of the impassive women in pale blue housecoats.

Charles may have been sinking under the hypnosis
of Mrs Routledge's endless talk, but he had enough
will left to recognise an opening for his investigation.
'You say Heather rings you every lunchtime?'

'Every lunchtime, without fail.'

'So I dare say she's told you a bit about the video
we've been doing?'

'Oh yes, all the details.'

'And I expect she rang you the day we were filming
in the warehouse a few weeks back... ?'

'Oh yes, she did. She was on for a long time. I remember the day, because it was later that I heard
about the dreadful accident to the poor girl who was
in the film. Do you know, she was playing the part
Heather would have been doing?'

'Well, yes, I—'

'And I kept thinking afterwards, if Heather had
actually been doing it, then she would have been the
one who had the accident.'

'I'm not sure that—'

'But wasn't it dreadful for that girl? A lot of that machinery they use isn't properly tested, you know. They've had other accidents here. There was a young man in one of the hoppers who...'

Heather had made contact with an impassive woman in a pale blue housecoat. The hot water was being procured. Charles hadn't got long.

'That day, Mrs Routledge,' he interrupted firmly, '—the day of the accident—do you remember what time Heather rang you?'

The old woman was so unused to being asked direct questions that she replied instinctively. 'Yes, I do. It was just before half-past twelve. I know, because I'd been listening to *You and Yours* on Radio Four—it's a good programme, that—and then they'd started with one of those new shows they keep trying to do with young comedians and bad language, and I don't hold with that—there's enough muck in the world without putting it on the wireless—and just after I'd switched off, Heather phoned.'

'And how long were you on the phone?'

The direct questioning really seemed to be working. Mrs Routledge replied, 'Oh, a good half-hour, because they'd just done the news headlines at one when I switched the wireless back on again.'

'And did Heather say whether there was anyone with her while she was talking to you?'

'Anyone with her?'

'Anyone else in the office?'

'Well, Brian—that's Mr Tressider—he came in, about one it must've been, because Heather said he'd come in and that's why she had to ring off. We've known Brian a long time, you know. He used to work here in Stenley Curton and at one time I hoped—'

Heather was moving back towards them with a pot of hot water, so Charles cut short Mrs Routledge's reminiscence. 'But Heather didn't say there was anyone there during the rest of the conversation?'

'No, no, of course not.' The old woman was only momentarily puzzled by this. Sensing a silence to be filled, she launched off again into her monologue. 'No, we've known Brian Tressider since he was a boy. He went to a school near here which . . .'

Heather looked at Charles curiously as she put the pot down. He looked equally curiously back at her.

What she was thinking he couldn't know. What he was thinking changed the whole premise of his investigation.

Mrs Routledge may have confirmed her daughter's alibi for the time of the murder, but she had virtually destroyed Trevor's. Heather had said the operator had been in her office at the relevant time, but surely he wouldn't have stood there for half an hour listening to Heather's minimal reactions to her mother maundering on.

So, if Trevor hadn't been in her office, where had he been? And, more importantly, why had she said he was there?

What possible motive could Heather Routledge have for lying to protect Trevor?

NINE

CHARLES FELT heavily ballasted with Jam Roly-Poly as he walked out of the canteen. Spending much time round Delmoleen, he realised, would have a devastating effect on his waistline (though, actually, these days it was more a general area than a precise line). Presumably, most of the people who used the canteen were manual workers who'd burn it all off pretty quickly; for actors the task might be more difficult.

Of course he didn't have to eat so substantially. Among the bays of the food counter there had been a salad bar, but, though Charles enjoyed salad as a garnish to a meal, he'd never been able to think of it as a meal in itself. Though capable of going without food for long periods if necessary—as, for instance, during the innumerable technical runs of plays that his career had encompassed—if given the chance to eat, Charles Paris liked to have a proper meal. And for him a meal didn't feel proper unless there was a slab of meat in the middle of it. Ideally, it should also have alcoholic accompaniment, though, if indulged at lunchtime, that did tend to make him a little dozy in the afternoon.

The Delmoleen canteen had deprived him of alcohol, but he doubted whether anything would have subdued his excitement that afternoon.

The information he had gathered from Mrs Routledge represented a big breakthrough in the murder investigation. With Trevor's alibi shot to pieces, the possible scenario which had led up to Dayna Richman's death had altered radically. Putting on one side for a moment the reasons for Heather's behaviour, Charles Paris now had to find out more about the forklift operator's actions that fateful lunchtime.

And that meant paying another visit to the warehouse.

ON HIS WAY across from the canteen, Charles met a very excited Will Parton. The excitement was in part due to the fact that the Delmoleen Executive dining room—unlike the canteen—did include alcohol amongst its privileges, but it had a second, more important, cause.

'Got another job, Charles,' the writer said gleefully.

'Oh yes?'

'Met Robin Pritchard in the Executive dining room.'

'You know all the stars, don't you?'

'Anyway, Biscuits and Cereals are launching a new product—very exciting, going to be very *big* . . .'

'With *global* outreach, no doubt?'

'You said it, Charles. It's going to be launched to the sales force at the sales conference in September, and he wants me to organise the presentation.'

'Just you as a writer, or is this a *Parton Parcel* job?'

'*Parton Parcel*. I mean, obviously I will write everything, but I get to direct it as well, if I want to—or bring in an outside director or . . . well, the possibilities are infinite.'

'This going to be another video job?'

'Could be. I'm having a meeting with Robin to sort out the nitty-gritty next week. At the moment we're thinking about a live kind of revue format, possibly with a slide presentation backing it up...we might add a video element, though...details to be sorted out, as I say. But it's a big, solid job—keep me busy for quite a while.'

'So the play gets deferred yet again?'

Will Parton looked pained. 'Got to go where the work is, Charles love.'

'Oh yes. You don't have to tell me that.'

'No.'

'And of course, if there is a role in the presentation for a speaking forklift truck operator...or indeed anything else...I'm a very versatile actor, you know... Forty-eight, but play younger...?'

'I'll bear it in mind, see if there is anything,' said Will loftily. He was rather enjoying the impresario role. His dismissiveness of Charles was revenge for years and years of working as a journeyman in television, endlessly rewriting, doing exactly what directors told him all the time. Through his involvement in *Parton Parcel* and the corporate videos, Will Parton was achieving a taste of that magic possession so rarely granted to writers—power.

'Are you going to the station, Charles?'

'Will be shortly. When's the next train?'

The writer, in his new hyper-efficient producer mode, had such facts at his fingertips. 'Two thirty-seven.'

'Oh, well, we've got a bit of time. Just someone I want to have a word with, so...see you on the platform?'

Will Parton looked at his friend wryly. 'You're not still off on this murder investigation routine, are you?'

'Well . . .' Charles shrugged awkwardly and made a hasty change of subject. 'What is this new product Robin Pritchard's launching?'

'Oh, couldn't tell you that, Charles. Bound to secrecy.' Will dropped into the earnest tones of the Product Manager. 'But I can tell you it's going to be very *big*.'

'Look, I'm not going to pass it on to anyone. No one I know gives a damn about new departures in the wonderful world of foodstuffs.'

'Ah, you may think that, Charles, but can't be too careful.'

'What you're actually saying, Will, is that you don't know what it is yet, do you?'

The writer was only momentarily discomfitted. 'That I'm afraid I can't reveal. But if the information had been kept from me, there would be good reasons for it.' He looked around elaborately and hissed, 'Industrial espionage—their spies are everywhere.'

'Come off it.'

'True. Lot of other companies desperate to increase their market share. If they found out about a new launch at this stage, it'd give them time to develop their own rival products.'

'Does it really work like that?'

'You betcha.' Will Parton winked conspiratorially. 'Biscuits and Cereals is a crumby business, Charles.'

THE FORKLIFTS in the warehouse were plying their endless trade, loading up with pallets from the shelves and carrying them across to the insatiable lorries.

No one seemed to notice Charles's entrance. The Delmoleen overalls had been shed, so perhaps his 'Trevor' costume helped him melt into the scenery. More likely, the operators on their trucks were concentrating too hard on their work to see the newcomer.

He cast a quick glance at the outer office, but it was empty. Heather was either in the back room or, more likely, still suffering her mother's monody of irrelevances.

The aisle where Dayna had died was empty. At its end once again there was a pile of empty pallets, though probably the original stack had been removed and another accumulated in the weeks since the incident.

Charles moved softly down the aisle. He knew it was ridiculous to hope that anything might still remain in the cavity between the pallets and the wall, but he was now fully psyched up and had to prove it by the evidence of his own eyes.

The hum of the forklifts and the occasional raucous shout from their operators sounded very distant.

He came to the end of the aisle and, with a quick look to either side, moved forward to the pallets.

'What the hell are you doing?'

Charles whirled round and found himself face to face with Trevor, who had just emerged from the end of the adjacent aisle. Whether he had been monitoring Charles's progress since the actor came into the warehouse or had just appeared at that moment by coincidence was impossible to know.

But the operator looked very mean. From his hand dangled one of the crowbars that was used for raising the lids of crates.

Charles said nothing as Trevor advanced towards him.

'Why're you snooping around?'

'We're here doing some more work on the video,' Charles's dry mouth managed to reply.

'That's in the canteen. No reason why you should be in here.'

'No. I just wanted to have a look around.'

Trevor tapped the crowbar on his open palm. 'Well, nobody wants people like you looking around.'

Charles tried to brazen it out. 'Perhaps not, but I want to do it. I still want to know what happened to Dayna Richman.'

'She died. There was an accident with a forklift truck and she died. If you hadn't left the truck switched on, she'd still be alive.'

'I didn't leave the truck switched on.'

'Don't try and be clever with me.' Trevor moved closer, close enough for Charles to smell the stale cigarette smoke on his breath. 'Just mind your own bloody business and get out of here—otherwise you're going to get hurt.' The crowbar was menacingly half-raised.

'You wouldn't dare hurt me in here. I'd shout. Someone'd hear me.'

Trevor let out a short bark of laughter. He jerked his head back towards the forklifts. 'Everyone here's a mate of mine. None of them have got much time for bleeding wankers like actors. If I want to hurt you, nobody's going to stop me.'

'Listen,' said Charles, sounding calmer than he felt, 'I want some information from you.'

'Oh yes? And what makes you think I'm going to give you any information?'

'To clear your name.'

'My name doesn't need clearing. Dayna's death was an accident, unfortunate combination of circumstances, the enquiry said. No individual to blame.'

'But the enquiry was just a cover-up.'

Trevor shrugged. 'Prove it.'

'Listen,' Charles said again, trying to assert himself, 'I don't think Dayna's death was an accident.'

'Oh no? What was it then?'

'Murder.'

'Really? Well, as I just said—you just try and prove it.'

'What's more,' Charles went on recklessly, 'I think you are the one who killed her.'

The attack came so quickly he had no time to defend himself. He felt the neck of his T-shirt grabbed so that the collar closed round his neck like a noose. At the same moment Trevor's knee smashed up into Charles's balls.

He supposed he should have been grateful that the crowbar hadn't been used, but, in the eye-watering agony of that moment, he thought he would have preferred it.

Trevor's smoky breath was right up against Charles's face as the voice hissed, 'Don't you dare ever say that again! You repeat that and there will be a murder done! And you'll be the one whose body never gets found! You breathe another word about—'

'Trevor,' said an authoritative voice from behind Charles, 'what the hell do you think you're doing?'

CHARLES HAD FORGOTTEN just how much a knee in the balls could hurt. His life, though shadowed by alcohol, had included surprisingly little drunken brawling, and he had to think back to playground fights of his schooldays for comparable injuries. But he had no problem in recognising the pain.

The trouble was, the way it made him walk instantly identified the cause of his problem, and he'd found the short trip from the warehouse to the office of his saviour, Ken Colebourne, extremely embarrassing. Delmoleen workers—both male and, to his surprise and mortification, female—provided a range of ready, if unoriginal, witticisms as he passed.

In the office—thank God—the Marketing Director kept a secret supply of liquor, and a couple of medicinal brandies slightly dulled the grinding agony in Charles's testicles—so long as he didn't try to do anything clever, like moving. He felt a sudden, totally irrational desire to sneeze, and prayed that he would be able to control it.

On the other side of the desk, Ken Colebourne looked serious. 'I'm extremely sorry about what's happened, Charles, but I'd really be grateful if you could keep quiet about it.'

Yes, of course. The Delmoleen name mustn't be tarnished by any adverse publicity. The company must be kept smelling of roses, just as it had been after Dayna's death.

As it happened, Charles didn't want any enquiries into what he had been doing to provoke Trevor's attack, so he had no intention of making a fuss. He told Ken as much.

The Marketing Director didn't look totally reassured. 'It really is very important that this is kept quiet.'

'Don't worry. It will be.'

'Good.' But a note of doubt remained in his voice. 'Why did you want to talk to Trevor?'

'I didn't. I was just down there, and he started talking to me.'

'I'd keep well away from him if I were you. He's a nasty piece of work. Can be quite violent.'

Charles made the mistake of moving. 'You don't have to tell me,' he agreed through gritted teeth.

'No.' Ken still seemed uncertain, as if there was something else, some further reassurance, he wanted from Charles. 'If you had been thinking of having any dealings with Trevor,' he went on awkwardly, 'I'd give up the idea. It won't do you any good. You won't get anything out of him. He's trouble, you know.'

'I do know.'

'Hm.' But the Marketing Director couldn't leave the subject alone. 'You weren't asking him about what he and Dayna got up to, were you?'

'No. As I say, he just came up to me and started getting aggressive. I think he was probably still miffed that I was substituted for him in the video.'

Ken Colebourne nodded, not believing the explanation any more than Charles did. 'Yes, that was probably it. Anyway, as I say, Charles, I'd leave it. Difficult for an outsider to understand quite how things work in a place like Delmoleen. I'd just steer clear of Trevor and forget the whole business, if I were you.'

Charles nodded. That was unwise; the movement jolted right through his body and ripples of pain lapped outwards from his groin.

The Marketing Director looked at his watch. 'You going to be all right to get back on the train? I could lay on a car for you if you like.'

'Oh, I'll be fine.' Then Charles thought of the glee-ful pleasantries with which Will Parton was likely to greet his affliction. The prospect of the writer's wit working overtime all the way to St Pancras was more than he could face. He winced. 'Well, actually, if you wouldn't mind...'

Ken Colebourne got on the phone to his secretary and organised transport. He proffered more brandy. Charles was at first inclined to refuse, but then thought, what the hell, I'm not going to be in any state to do anything else today, may as well succumb. He allowed his glass to be generously filled, without wor-rying about the fact that he'd almost definitely move on to the whisky when he got back to Hereford Road. He'd cross that hangover when he came to it.

'So I have your word that you won't mention this to anyone?' Ken insisted.

'No problem. Forgotten all about it already.'

Charles was intrigued by the man's over-reaction. Again it suggested some involvement in the affairs of Trevor and Dayna, and stimulated rather than al-layed suspicion.

What the Marketing Director said next stimulated it even more. 'And if there's any favour I can do for you that'll help you forget the whole business, well, you only have to say the word...'

This was so unexpected that it took Charles a moment to realise he was being offered a bribe. 'Favour?' he echoed stupidly.

'Yes.' Ken Colebourne wasn't finding these negotiations particularly easy, but he was managing without total embarrassment, which suggested it wasn't the first time he'd made such offers.

'I wasn't talking money, of course, though it might be possible for some kind of arrangement to be made on those lines. But I was thinking more of... well, maybe some kind of event you'd like to attend...?'

'Event?'

'I have a lot of dealings with public relations companies. Most things can be arranged these days. The unobtainable has become very obtainable if you know who to ask.'

'What kind of unobtainable?'

'Well, concerts, theatre, opera tickets, those'd be no problem, whatever show you wanted to see. I can pick up the phone now and get you seats for tonight at the hottest show in the West End.'

'Oh?'

'Or, of course, if it's sport that interests you... well, you name it. Test matches, rugby internationals, Ascot, golf, Wimbledon, Henley, whatever you fancy... And I'm not just talking tickets here, I'm talking executive hospitality—you know, the full package. A really good day.'

'Ah.' Charles, so unused to being courted in this way, was lost for the right response.

'I mean, what I'm saying is that I do very much appreciate the way you've taken this incident...' Ken Colebourne spelled out the deal, 'you know, saying you'll forget all about it, not take it any further... so I'd like to say a little thank-you to you in some appropriate way. Bit of a quid pro quo if you like...'

'I see.'

'So what do you say? Anything in the little lot I've mentioned that might maybe appeal to you...?'

Charles had never had to ask himself before whether or not he was corruptible. By custom, the subjects of bribery are people who wield power and influence. There's never been much percentage in trying to corrupt a predominantly out-of-work actor.

So the ethical dilemma that faced him was unfamiliar.

He certainly had no intention of abandoning his murder investigation. But Ken Colebourne had talked in such veiled terms that it wasn't at all certain that that was what was being asked.

On balance, Charles decided that accepting one of the offers would not be compromising himself at all. At the very least, he deserved some compensation for his bruised testicles.

And, besides, there was one entertainment on Ken's list that did appeal a great deal.

It didn't actually appeal much to Charles Paris himself.

But he knew someone it really would appeal to.

He asked Ken Colebourne to make the arrangements.

TEN

'FRANCES, IT'S ME.'

'Ah.'

'We're getting predictable.'

'What do you mean?'

'I keep ringing up and saying "Frances, it's me" and you keep saying "Ah".'

'So?'

'So nothing. I just mention it in passing.'

'Ah.'

'There's another one.'

'Mm. How are you then? All right?'

'Well, I am suffering a bit because someone kneed me in the balls.'

'Perhaps that'll teach you to stop chasing young girls.'

'It wasn't anything like that. It was...oh, never mind. Look, Frances, you remember when we last spoke...?'

'How could I forget it? You rang up and said "Frances, it's me" and I said "Ah".'

'Yes. But on that occasion we also agreed that when I next rang up it should be with an invitation to something nice that you might like to do.'

'I'm not sure that we agreed it. I said it'd be nice. I don't recall you being that enthusiastic.'

'Well, be that as it may. The thing is, I am now ringing to invite you out to something nice that I think you'll enjoy.'

'Oh yes? When?'

'Saturday week.'

'What time?'

'Late morning till early evening.'

'Ah.'

'That's another "Ah", Frances. And, you know, the intonation of your "Ahs" is getting increasingly deterrent.'

'Yes. The thing is, Charles, that that Saturday is the middle Saturday of Wimbledon.'

'I know.'

'Well, if you know that, then you should also know that I get totally hooked during the Wimbledon fortnight and spend every spare moment glued to the television.'

'I do know that. That's the point.'

'What's the point?'

'The point is that I want to drag you away from watching Wimbledon on the television . . .'

'But it's one of the things I really enjoy!'

'. . . and take you to watch Wimbledon in the flesh.'

'Where?'

'At Wimbledon.'

'Oh. Charles, you're not suggesting that you and I, at our age, drag ourselves over to Wimbledon in the early morning and queue for hours to—?'

'No, Frances, I am saying I have two tickets to an executive hospitality suite at Wimbledon for that Saturday, and I am asking whether you would do me the honour of accompanying me there as my guest?'

'Ah.'

'Now that's a much nicer "Ah", Frances.'

'CHARLES, BIT OF A CRISIS.'

'What kind of crisis, Will?'

'Got a meeting with Robin Pritchard at eleven-thirty tomorrow morning. About this new product. With him and the account executive from the ad agency. Thing is, Seb Ormond was going to go along with me.'

'Why?'

'As set-dressing, really. Told you I don't want them to get the impression that *Parton Parcel* is just a one-man band.'

'But it is just a one-man band, isn't it?'

'Of course it is, but that's not the point. Having Seb sitting there looking dourly executive in his suit gives the set-up a bit of . . . I don't know . . .'

'*Gravitas.*'

'The very word. Anyway, Seb's cried off. Bugger's going to Manila for a new washing machine.'

'Seems a long way to go for a washing machine.'

'Don't be deliberately obtuse, Charles. He's presenting the launch of a new washing machine out there . . . you know, standing up, reading from an autocue and getting paid a fortune for his pains.'

'All right for some.'

'Anyway, thing is, it puts me in a bit of a spot.'

'Lack of *gravitas*, you mean?'

'That's it. You see, I want my set-up to look like a heavy-duty, solid company, so I can't turn up to a big meeting on my own.'

'I don't quite see why.'

'You take my word for it, I can't. I know these people. Numbers count with them. So, Charles, reason I'm ringing is I wondered if you might be free to come along with me tomorrow . . . ?'

'Oh. Well, Will, I'm very flattered that I'm the person you first thought of.'

'Of course you're not the person I first thought of! Nobody else was free.'

'Oh.'

'Come on, will you do it?'

'*I* might not be free,' said Charles loftily.

'Don't be ridiculous, Charles. You're always free. Come on, help me out of a spot.' There was a silence. 'If you do, I'll see that there's something for you at the sales conference in Brighton . . .'

The bribe of work had its usual, instantaneous effect. Charles agreed to go to the meeting.

'But what will I have to do?'

'Nothing.'

'Nothing?'

'No, just sit there holding a briefcase and look like you're making a mental note of everything that's being said.'

'Why?'

'It'll intimidate them a bit. Always a good idea to have one person at a meeting who doesn't say anything—it makes all the others terribly self-conscious about what *they*'re saying. And raises the *gravitas* quotient.'

'Ah. Right. But isn't Robin Pritchard going to think it's odd, me being there? I mean, he last saw me as a forklift truck operator. I don't think forklift truck operators have a particularly high *gravitas* quotient.'

'Don't worry. He'll be seeing you in a different context. I'll tell him you're part of the *Parton Parcel* set-up and that that's why you did the first job. It won't be a problem.'

'If you say so. What voice shall I use?'

Charles rather fancied using that one he'd developed for Thomas Cromwell for *A Man For All Seasons* at Worthing ('This play is as well-made as a mahogany sideboard, and the acting was matchingly wooden'—*West Sussex Gazette*). Or possibly his Sir Benjamin Backbite from that Cheltenham *School for Scandal* ('The only scandal about this dire production was that Arts Council money helped to fund it'—*Gloucester Citizen*).

But such speculation was quickly curbed by Will. 'I told you, you don't say anything.'

'But—'

'And if you do have to say anything, you use your own voice.'

'Oh. OK.' He couldn't pretend he wasn't a little disappointed.

'And, again, no giggling.'

'Promise.'

'One other thing, Charles . . .'

'Yes.'

'Suit.'

'Ah.' Then, hopefully, 'You don't think the suit I've got could be—'

'Charles . . .' The intonation said it all.

'No. I see. Right.'

'Point is, actually, if you're going to be doing much more corporate work . . .'

'Yes?'

'Which you do want to, don't you . . . ?'

'Oh, yes, yes, sure.' The reply was instinctive. It wasn't particularly corporate work he wanted to do, just work.

'Well, it really is about time you started building up your wardrobe. I mean, for every time you're asked to do a forklift truck operator, you're going to be offered ten executives.'

'Hm. So what you're saying, Will, is that I'm going to have to buy a suit?'

'That's exactly what I'm saying.'

'And before this meeting?'

'Right.'

Charles was torn. Buying a suit was unbelievably low on his list of priorities. On the other hand, if that investment was the necessary key to a whole new field of lucrative work... 'OK, Will, I'll buy one in the morning. Where is the meeting? Out at Stenley Curton?'

'No, it's in London. But, Charles, we must meet before the meeting.'

'What, you need to brief me?'

'Good heavens, no. But you don't think I trust you to buy a suit on your own, do you?'

THEY MET, AS ARRANGED, at Oxford Circus. Charles was a bit vague about where to go from there. 'John Lewis pretty safe, isn't it? Or Marks & Spencers sell suits these days, don't they?'

He thought he was doing rather well, given how long it had been since he made a comparable purchase. Two ideas for where to go straight away—not bad. But the expression on Will Parton's face told him that he was not doing well at all.

'For heaven's sake, Charles, we're dressing an up-to-the-minute executive here, not a Leader of the Labour Party.'

'What do you mean?'

'We're after something with a bit of *style*.'

'Oh, come on, a suit's a suit, isn't it?'

'No, it isn't.' Will slid into his 'affected artist' voice. 'A suit's like a theatrical performance, love—it can look as if it's been totally grafted on from the outside, or it can flow from within so that one cannot tell where the personality stops and the suit begins.'

'Oh, my God.' Charles was reminded of an occasion in the sixties. He had been in Stratford, wearing a former suit, an ancient voluminous garment in fuzzy charcoal tweed inherited from his father, and had met an actor wearing a collarless Beatle-style number in identical fabric.

'Look,' Charles had said, holding his sleeve against the other actor's, 'same material.'

'Yes,' the actor had responded waspishly, 'but I had a *suit* made out of mine.'

Will hailed a cab and took Charles to Covent Garden. There he led him into a long narrow shop. The graphics over the door were so trendily minimalist that Charles couldn't read what the place was called. Once inside, Will showed a determination to kit his friend out as a minor *mafioso*.

'Surely this is too big,' whispered Charles, as he shambled out of the changing booth in a slightly shiny striped ensemble, which hung off him like the skin of an elephant six weeks into a crash diet.

'He thinks it's too big,' said Will, gleefully cruel.

'It is the *style*,' said the razor-thin shop assistant, with a waspishness which raised the possibility that his father might have worked at Stratford in the sixties.

'Feels quite lightweight, too,' Charles persisted. 'I like a suit with a bit of bulk. You know, for the winter. Got to keep warm.'

'It's summer,' said the young man, with a contemptuous flick of his pony-tail.

'Yes, but got to think ahead.'

'And since most offices these days are air-conditioned, today's executive tends to favour the lighter fabric.'

'Oh.'

'And have a topcoat to wear outside when the weather's cold.'

'Ah.'

'We do have an extensive range of topcoats if you—'

'Ah, er, no, thank you,' said Charles, who had just caught a glimpse of the price ticket on the suit. He looked across at Will and flapped his arms like an apologetic penguin. 'What do you think?'

'Hm. It's a bit *sober*, isn't it?'

'*Sober*?'

The writer turned maliciously to a hanging suit in pale flecked tweed, whose effect was of home-made cream of mushroom soup with croutons in it. 'This makes a bit more of a statement, doesn't it?'

Charles scotched that idea very quickly. 'Yes, but it's a statement from which I would firmly wish to dissociate myself, thank you very much.'

They ummed and erred. The young man wondered whether the gentleman would look better in a light herringbone (but in a defeated tone which implied he didn't really think the gentleman would look better in anything).

Charles took another look at himself in the mirror. He pulled the looseness of the double-breasted jacket away from his stomach. 'At least this is quite flattering to the fuller figure,' he chuckled.

'No, actually, sir,' said the young man, 'the style does look rather better on someone with a proper figure.'

'Oh well, perhaps I should be shopping for a new figure rather than a new suit,' Charles suggested, with a grin.

'Wouldn't be a bad idea,' the young man murmured, fingering one of his earrings.

'That one's a good fit,' said Will. 'Gives you a bit of edge, certainly.'

'Is "edge" what we're looking for?' asked Charles cautiously.

Will glanced at his watch. 'We haven't got too long to piss about. I think we should go for it, Charles.'

'Well, if you're sure—'

'Yes, we'll have it.'

'If that's your decision,' sighed the young man, in the manner of someone whose recommendation that Caesar stay at home on the Ides of March had just been overruled.

'Right, you'd better keep it on, Charles. Oh no, first you need a shirt and tie.'

'I'm wearing a shirt and tie.'

Protest was vain. He was dragged over to another display and kitted out with a soft cotton shirt whose sleeves were puffy enough to play Hamlet in, and a silk tie with a design that Braque might have knocked up and rejected while prostrated by flu. The tie, he noticed, cost as much as the last suit he had bought.

Paying was a problem. Charles had just achieved the unachievable and, following an ugly sequence of threatening letters, managed to pay off the debts on both his credit cards. At that unaccustomed moment of solvency, he had resolved to impose on himself a rigid regime of economy. That this intention was serious can be judged from the fact that he even— briefly—contemplated counting, and if necessary rationing, the number of bottles of Bell's whisky he bought.

Still, the road to hell is paved with plastic. He drew out the card and once again plunged deep, deep into debt.

He tried to convince himself that the clothes were a valuable investment for his career, but natural cynicism made such casuistry impossible.

While he changed into the shirt and tie, the shop assistant bundled his old clothes into a plastic carrier, which he placed on the floor behind the counter.

'Could I have those, please?' asked Charles, as he was about to leave.

'Good heavens,' murmured the young man, lifting his eyes to heaven. 'You mean you want to *keep* them?'

ELEVEN

CHARLES PARIS felt an absolute prune as he walked into the Delmoleen Knightsbridge offices. The shiny material of his new suit flapped irritatingly around him. Surely, not since the days of Demobilisation, had anyone walked around in clothes so patently the wrong size.

He was reassured, however, in the conference room where they met, to discover that Robin Pritchard and the agency man were dressed in almost identical garb, suits hanging in folds around them, bright silk ties progressing uneasily from Cubism to Surrealism. And when he actually came to look at Will, he saw that the writer was wearing much the same uniform. So, though Charles Paris still felt a prune, he was at least at a convention of prunes.

Certainly Robin Pritchard made no indication of their having met before, even though Charles was introduced by the same name. This was probably just professional discretion on the Product Manager's part, though Charles couldn't help wondering whether the suit transformed him so totally that it expunged all memory of his former forklift operator persona.

Robin Pritchard started by saying how very *big* the new product was going to be, how *huge* its launch campaign would be, how *global* its likely outreach, and how *massively* it was going to increase Delmoleen's brand share in that particular market.

Charles Paris sat through all this looking properly executive, the neat briefcase Will had supplied beside him, trying to give the impression that its contents were something of more significance than his old clothes. But his mind was wandering.

He took in the expansive sparseness of the conference room, which was of a piece with the rest of the Delmoleen Head Office. The reception area and corridors were all light grey, with flecked grey carpets. Desks were of darker grey, while low sofas and armchairs were delicately pink, like the underside of a trout. A few discreetly expensive abstract paintings hung on the walls.

There was nothing about the place that obviously said Delmoleen. Compared to the Stanley Curton site with its huge logos, or Ken Colebourne's office decorated with product pictures, the Knightsbridge premises were reticently anonymous. Only a small steel plate on their portico mentioned the Delmoleen name. They could have been the headquarters of an insurance company, an advertising agency, a merchant bank, a hotel chain, anything.

Presumably it was here that Brian Tressider had his office and spent most of his time. Charles wondered idly whether the Delmoleen video would include shooting at the London end. There wasn't much chance of his being required if it did. The London-based executives were probably capable of speaking for themselves and, though he did now possess the right suit for a managerial role, his facial similarity to the speaking forklift operator might not pass undetected.

His mind came back to Dayna Richman's murder—came back rather guiltily, it must be said. He had been trying not to think about it for the last few weeks. It wasn't the memory of Trevor's knee in his crotch that put him off, nor was he deferring in response to Ken Colebourne's bribery—it was just that he didn't know how to proceed on the case. Without any good reason to return to Stenley Curton, it was hard to continue the investigation.

And, in a way, the investigation was complete. Charles Paris was convinced that Trevor had killed Dayna, though he couldn't precisely define the man's motive. Presumably, sex was at the bottom of it somewhere. It usually was when a man and a woman were involved. A lovers' tiff, something along those lines... Anyway, the prospect of finding any proof of what had actually happened seemed ever more remote.

'And the really important, revolutionary, mould-breaking thing about the product is that it's *green*.'

Robin Pritchard's pronouncement brought Charles back to the present with a jolt. The Product Manager looked triumphant. The agency man, who already knew what the product was, shook his head in benign amazement at the boldness of its concept. Will Parton, who didn't yet know what the product was, looked as impressed as only someone pitching for a lucrative contract can.

They all turned to Charles Paris for his reaction. He decided that an expression of awestruck reverence would be appropriate and, since they all looked away with satisfaction, presumably he had got it right.

'Now when I say *green*,' Robin Pritchard continued, 'obviously I'm using the word in the environmental sense...'

'Obviously,' Will Parton agreed.

'So all the ingredients will have been organically
grown, and not only will they—the ingredients—be
listed on the wrapper, but their provenance will also be
detailed—you know, to show that they have been
processed in a way that has done the minimum harm
to the environment...'

Will, who Charles had heard on many occasions say
that he didn't give a damn about the environment so
long as he had a fridge that worked, nodded enthusiastic endorsement of Robin Pritchard's words.

'What is more, the wrapper will be made from
wholly recycled paper and be coloured by pigments
that are totally biodegradable. Not only that, but for
every unit sold, a sum of money will be donated to an
environmental charity—you know, to replace some of
the rainforest, do something for the ozone layer,
whatever...'

'How much?'

'How much?'

'Yes, how much will be given to the environmental
charity?'

Will's question seemed to fluster the Product Manager. 'Well, the precise, er...the precise details are yet
to be worked out. I mean, we are talking a percentage
here, and inevitably a fairly small percentage—'

'But the purchasers needn't know that,' the agency
man chipped in smugly. 'The campaign will empha-
sise the *fact* of the donation rather than the precise
amount.'

'Exactly,' said Robin, 'but, nonetheless, given the number of product units we are hoping to shift, we are talking a very considerable sum of money.'

'Certainly, certainly,' the agency man conceded magnanimously. 'And the environmental value of the product will obviously be stressed at every point of the campaign.'

'And so,' said Will, 'every unit that's sold, for the rest of time, will be raising money for the environment.'

'Well, no, not *for the rest of time*,' said Robin Pritchard cautiously. 'I mean, we do obviously have to think of our profit margins. No, the donations will be made only over the initial three-month period of the launch.'

'And then they'll stop?'

'Yes, in effect they will. I mean, you can't go on doing that kind of thing for ever. Delmoleen's not a charity, you know.'

'Of course not.'

'But again,' the agency man chipped in, 'while our campaign will stress the donation element over the launch period, it would not be of interest to anyone for us to make too much of a song and dance about the moment when that element is dropped.'

'No, of course not,' Will Parton concurred.

'So, as you'll have gathered, this thing is going to be really *big*. What do you say, Will?'

'Certainly sounds *big*, Robin. And very exciting.'

'Charles?'

He didn't quite know the correct response. Will had told him to say nothing, but to do so to a direct question seemed downright rude. So he just shook his head in astonished disbelief and said, '*Big*.'

Robin Pritchard nodded, gratified, but Charles couldn't help adding, 'Sorry, you haven't said what the product is yet... ?'

'It's the Delmoleen "Green",' the Product Manager announced momentously.

'Ah.' Charles nodded. 'Green what?'

'It's just called the "Green". That's the beauty of the name, its sheer, minimalist simplicity.'

'Yes. Yes, of course. But what is it? Is it a breakfast cereal or a biscuit or a... ?'

'Oh, right. With you, Charles.' Robin Pritchard pursed his lips. 'The Delmoleen "Green" is such a revolutionary concept in biscuitry that it's very hard to define. I guess the nearest existing product to what we're talking about here is a muesli bar.'

'A muesli bar?'

'Right. The Delmoleen "Green" has all the virtues of the traditional muesli bar...' (Charles found it difficult to imagine that muesli bars had been around long enough to have their own traditions) '...and those of the current "State of the Art" muesli bar— I'm talking 100 per cent natural ingredients, high wholegrain dietary fibre content, low sugar, low saturated fat, the obvious stuff... The Delmoleen "Green" has all that and a bit more—but it also has the special feature which is going to take it rocketing to the top of the Crunch Bar and Snack Biscuit Brand Share.'

'What's that?' asked Will Parton, dead on cue.

'It's green,' Robin Pritchard whispered reverentially.

'Green?'

'Yes, 100 per cent green.'

Charles Paris, confused, couldn't stop himself from saying, 'But you said that. You said it was green. It's called the Delmoleen "Green"—'

'And it's green.'

'Ah.' That still didn't clarify things much for Charles.

But the Product Manager's next words did. 'It is green in colour. Green like Nature, green like little green apples, green like the leaves of spring, green like...' He ran out of poetic inspiration, 'green like—green. Coloured, of course, from natural dyes, the Delmoleen "Green" will be the only product in the entire *global* muesli bar range that it is actually coloured green.'

An impressed silence ensued.

Then, tentatively and sycophantically, Will Parton asked, 'You don't mean that the wrapper will be green in colour too?'

'You said it,' a complacent Robin Pritchard confirmed. 'Now, is that marketing or is that marketing?'

Will Parton shook his head in slow, stunned amazement. 'I'd say that's marketing.'

The Product Manager smiled the kind of smile Tamburlaine might have allowed himself when he entered the vanquished Persepolis. He looked at his watch. 'Now we have a table booked for lunch to get down to the nuts and bolts of the launch, but before that I have a little surprise for you.'

'Oh?' they all said, elaborately wondering what it could be.

Silently Robin Pritchard pressed down the key of an intercom and murmured, 'Ready, Janice.'

The door opened and a smartly-suited secretary entered. She carried a silver salver. On it lay three rectangles of what looked like green fibre matting.

'No? It isn't?' asked Will (overacting a bit, in Charles's estimation).

'Yes, it is. You three will be the only people outside Delmoleen ever to have tasted a Delmoleen "Green".'

Appropriately honoured noises were made, as the girl handed around the sacred batons.

Among the many, many foodstuffs that Charles Paris enjoyed, muesli bars did not figure at any level. And a green muesli bar would, under normal circumstances, be something to be consigned instantly to the dustbin.

The idea of eating a green muesli bar immediately before lunch was even more disgusting.

But he, like Will Parton and the agency man, lifted one of the rectangles off the salver as if handling a Dead Sea Scroll.

And he, like the others, looked to Robin Pritchard for the inestimable gift of permission, which was conceded by a gracious nod of the head.

Charles Paris, Will Parton and the agency man lifted their Delmoleen "Green" to their mouths in unison. Together, they took the first bite. Together, they shook their heads discreetly from side to side as they tried to dislodge a chunk from the sticky whole. Together, they munched.

'Ah,' they all said together, 'wonderful.'

Or that was probably what they said. It was difficult to be sure because their teeth were a bit glued together.

THE LUNCH DID NOT hold much interest for Charles. The food was fine, good trattoria fare, but his enjoyment of it was marred by all the bits of green oats, nuts and other fibre stuck between his teeth.

Then there was the drinking problem.

'Now, what are we going to have to drink?' Robin Pritchard had asked bonhomously on arrival.

Charles's mouth was half-open before he caught the steel in Will Parton's eye. 'Mineral water for me,' said the writer firmly.

'Me too,' said the agency man.

'Charles?'

'Yes, mineral water. Sounds terrific.'

Ooh, it hurt. Not only because he'd really been promising himself a few nice glasses of nice wine, but because he so deeply hated mineral water. Charles Paris was not a party to the Perrier conspiracy. When he wanted water—and even he, occasionally, particularly if he woke parched in the middle of the night, did want water—he found the tap perfectly adequate to his needs. The idea of paying bubbled-up prices for bubbled-up water appalled him. Apart from anything else mineral water at lunchtime meant that all afternoon his stomach would rumble like a demented washing machine going into its final spin.

He thought wistfully of the business world Ken Colebourne had referred to with such nostalgia, when deals were thrashed out between friends over a few beers.

Still, Charles Paris was there solely to help Will secure the contract for *Parton Parcel*. Just as he had swallowed down every last crumb—and there did seem to be a lot of them—of the Delmoleen 'Green', so he would swallow down the mineral water. He was playing a part, after all. That thought, a direct appeal to his own professionalism, did bring a kind of comfort.

It wasn't difficult for him to maintain his pose of silence during the meal. Robin Pritchard went on and on about the brilliance of his product, the agency man went on and on about the brilliance of his ideas for its launch campaign, and Will Parton went on and on about the brilliant, though as yet unspecified, way in which he would present the Delmoleen 'Green' to the sales force at the Brighton conference in September.

Charles, trying to imagine how Seb Ormond would play his part, looked grave and deep and nodded thoughtfully a lot.

There was only one moment when the conversation caught his interest. Will was setting out his stall, expatiating on how brilliantly he had scripted the Delmoleen video, which brought up the subject of the day's shooting in the warehouse.

'Oh yes,' said Robin Pritchard. 'That was when the factory bike got crushed.'

'Factory bike?' queried Charles, as if he had never heard the expression.

'Used to describe a young lady who's—what shall we say?—generous with her favours?'

'Oh. So Dayna Richman had that reputation, did she?'

'Quite justified, from all accounts. Cut a swathe through the warehouse lads like the First World War, I gather.'

'Was Trevor one of the victims?'

'Trevor with the forklift?'

'Mm.'

'Good heavens, no. Trevor's gay.'

'Oh?' That was unexpected. On the other hand, it did explain the unidentified laugh which had greeted Trevor's reference to Charles as a 'bleeding fairy'.

Charles couldn't resist the follow-up question. 'You don't happen to know if she was going around with any of the other lads at the time she died, do you?'

'Wouldn't have thought so. Having tested out her basic skills and found everything in working order, I think young Dayna was aiming a bit more up-market.'

'What? Are you talking about anyone in particular or—?'

'*Charles* ...' Will Parton hissed with a veiled look of fury. 'Robin, about the actual sales conference ...'

Charles felt guilty. He mustn't screw up the deal for *Parton Parcel*. No, his murder investigation would have to go on hold yet again.

He would have to be content for the moment with the tiny fragment Robin Pritchard had given him.

The new information did put an intriguing new light on the situation, though.

TWELVE

'MY GOD, CHARLES, what on earth are you wearing?'

Frances stood aghast at the door of her flat.

'It is possible for me to look smart, you know,
Frances.'

'Smart? Is that smart? Have you got a part in *God-
father IV* or what?'

'I am just dressed as the young executive dresses
these days.'

'Since when have you been a young executive? I've
heard of mutton-dressed-as-lamb, but... My God,
Charles, what's that smell? It's not mint sauce, is it?'

'It's after-shave,' he confessed sheepishly (or mut-
ton-dressed-as-lambishly). Will had tipped him the
wink that some kind of 'man's fragrance' really was
required to complete the executive image.

'Good heavens.'

'Come on. The car's waiting.'

KEN COLEBOURNE had done them proud. Car to pick
up Charles in Bayswater, on to Highgate to collect
Frances, and then down through the traffic to Wimbledon.

'This is very exciting,' Frances said. 'Haven't actually been to Wimbledon for about ten years. Always
used to queue up and go in my teens, but in later life
being in charge of school parties rather took the gilt

off the experience. Spent all the time watching my charges rather than the tennis, seeing they weren't being picked up by randy young men or rubbed up by dirty old men. No, this really is wonderful.'

She looked terrific that morning. With age, Frances had managed to stay elegantly thin rather than turning stringy. She was neatly dressed in a generously-skirted navy suit and cream blouse with a big collar, an ensemble Charles hadn't seen before.

It was still a shock that he no longer knew his wife's wardrobe inside out, but that was one of the many rights he had given up by walking out on her all those years ago. Unreasonable though he knew the desire was, some part of Charles still felt she should consult him about the clothes she bought.

Though he wanted the freedom to vanish off her landscape for months on end, he couldn't quite reconcile himself to the idea of Frances leading a life of her own. Though he knew he was being a dog in the manger, a jealous arrogance kept telling him he really was the love of her life and, so long as he was alive, she'd never be truly independent.

Increasingly, though, the evidence was turning against him. Charles was hoist with his own petard. He had left Frances in the hope of attaining his own independence, but over the years she had proved much more adept at making a life of her own than he had.

He liked to think the mutual ties remained so strong, that, in spite of detours and diversions, the relationship was still central to both of them. And even that one day they'd get back together again.

But he was decreasingly convinced that Frances felt the same. The coolness that she had at first affected as a defence against him now seemed more instinctive.

'Juliet was so jealous when I told her where we were going. She still loves her tennis.'

'Oh. Right.' Charles had always intended to do more things, like play tennis, with his daughter while she was growing up, but he had been away a lot, and then of course he'd moved out, and suddenly she had been grown up and married and a mother three times over, and he had realised that his chance was gone and that Frances had been responsible for every aspect of Juliet's upbringing.

'I must get in touch with her,' he said contritely.

'Yes, you must,' Frances agreed with some asperity.

He looked sideways at her as the car negotiated the heavy traffic of Wimbledon High Street, and felt an ache of longing. He really must make a proper effort to get her back. Frances was too good to lose.

He knew he had had such intentions many times before, but they had always been diluted by lethargy or diverted by skirmishes with other women. When he was actually with Frances, it seemed inconceivable that he could ever fancy anyone else. But he recognised the volatility of the masculine character, that resurgent and shameful inability to meet any woman without thoughts of sex intruding; and he knew that, given the right circumstances, with Frances off the scene and someone else attractive to him on it, the whole process would start all over again.

But this time he really must put all irrelevant thoughts to one side, and work to regain Frances's affection. He felt a sudden stab of lust as he looked at her.

Greatly daring, Charles Paris put his hand on his wife's knee.

She didn't remove it. She looked straight into his eyes and smiled a warm smile of complicity.

That had to be a good sign.

IT WAS RATHER a good feeling to be whisked past the endless, patient lines of tennis fans to one of the main gates. Their driver sorted out a time and pick-up point for the end of the day's play, and gave them a phone number to call if any change was required to these arrangements. Their tickets were checked at the gate and, following the map in the neat information pack which Ken Colebourne had sent Charles, they made their way to the Delmoleen marquee.

As they walked through the crowds, Frances commented on how the atmosphere had changed since she'd last been there. 'There weren't all these booths and shops. There wasn't nearly so much for sale, I'm sure.'

Charles stopped by a display of clothes, indicating a green and purple track suit with 'The Championships—Wimbledon' logo. 'Like me to buy you one of these?'

'Not quite my style, Charles. But don't let me stop you getting one for yourself.'

'Don't think it's quite my style either.'

'I don't know, love. Now I've seen that suit, nothing you wear's going to surprise me.'

She put her arm in his. And she had called him 'love.' It was nice having a wife.

He felt this even more when they reached the Delmoleen marquee. Following the map, they had turned into an alley of corporate entertainment. There were rows of marquees on either side, fronted by neatly fenced-off areas with white chairs and round tables shaded by beach umbrellas. Men in suits and smartly dressed ladies stood sipping champagne in the various pens.

From the small signs on the entrances Charles recognised among the corporate entertainers a major bank, an insurance company and the BBC. On the forecourt of the BBC marquee stood various well-known television faces, pretending they weren't aware that everyone recognised them.

The Delmoleen marquee's number was clearly marked on the map and its entrance discreetly sign-posted by the company logo. Charles was glad he had Frances with him. Much easier to make an entrance into a crowd of strangers as a couple. There really was a lot to be said for marriage. Good system.

As it turned out, there were some faces he recognised. Brian and Brenda Tressider were there, so was Ken Colebourne, but he looked in vain for Robin Pritchard. Charles had rather hoped to see the Product Manager again and follow up on their last, incomplete conversation. However, it looked as though the murder investigation would have to remain on hold.

The other guests were smartly anonymous, presumably substantial customers or suppliers having their relationships with Delmoleen cemented and massaged by a corporate freebie. Charles had been a little worried that Brian Tressider might question his

right to be there, wondering what possible benefit
could accrue to the company from scratching the back
of an unemployed actor—even one supposed to have
some ill-defined connection with the *Parton Parcel*
production company. But of course the Managing
Director, whatever his true feelings on the matter, was
far too urbane to let them show.

Well-rehearsed on the guest-list, he effusively wel-
comed Charles and Frances, telling her that her husband had done excellent work on the video they were
making.

Brenda Tressider was equally punctilious, and her
social filing system did not let her down. 'Yes, of
course, Charles Paris, how delightful to see you again.
You entertained us so much in that splendid *Stanislas
Braid* series. It must be really strange seeing your husband on the television screen so often, Mrs Paris.'

'Well, it's not *that* often,' said Frances—rather
traitorously, to Charles's mind.

'Oh, but much more than the average wife. I mean,
I've seen Brian interviewed once or twice on business
programmes and it always gives me a very odd feeling. But I suppose, like most things, you get used to it.'
A uniformed waitress with a tray of champagne materialised at her elbow. 'Now do help yourself to a
drink, and let me introduce you to some people . . .'

They were impeccably introduced to everyone and
Charles found, as he usually did on these occasions,
that the names went straight in one ear and out the
other. So did all the useful background detail that
Brenda Tressider supplied for her guests. She was doing her job wonderfully, presenting innumerable
prompts to conversation; it wasn't her fault that

Charles Paris seemed incapable of retaining the information.

Frances was much better at this sort of thing than he was. She plunged instantly into conversation with one of the women about the latest American infant tennis sensation, and was quickly whirled away, leaving her husband stranded.

Charles stood grinning fatuously round a group of three couples, whose names and companies he had instantly forgotten. He sipped at his champagne, then took a longer swig. The waitress manifested herself once again beside him. He put down his empty glass and picked up a full one.

'What a lovely day for the tennis,' he said, opting to keep his remarks uncontroversial.

The three couples agreed it was a lovely day for the tennis.

'Yes, lovely day for the tennis,' Charles confirmed.

He had a sense of *déjà vu*. For a moment he couldn't place it, then recalled that he had spoken exactly that dialogue in one of those fifties french-window comedies about a publisher. (They had all been about publishers; to the dramatists of the time, publishing represented a lucrative profession whose demands were in no danger of impinging on anyone's private life.) Now what had the play been called . . . ? Oh yes, *Service Not Included*, he remembered it now.

He also, unfortunately, remembered the review the *Halifax Evening Courier* had given his performance. 'Charles Paris wanders dementedly through the play, like Van Gogh trying to decide which ear to cut off.'

He saw Ken Colebourne grinning and waving, and excused himself from further reaffirmation with the three couples of how good a day it was for tennis.

'All the arrangements went all right, did they?'

'Fine, Ken. Yes, very grateful to you for setting the whole thing up. My wife's absolutely delighted to be here. I must introduce you.'

'Well, first let me introduce you to my wife. Patricia dear, this is Charles Paris.'

The sight of Patricia Colebourne was quite a shock. He had hardly noticed her, lost in the shadows under one of the umbrellas. She was agonisingly thin; the beige linen dress hung slackly from the angularity of her shoulders; and her skin had a waxy pallor. Two sticks were hooked from the lip of the table.

She was clearly a very sick woman, and yet the formalities of introduction do not traditionally include a medical bulletin, so Charles could only shake the hand that felt like a bunch of dry twigs and say, 'Pleasure to meet you'.

'Patricia's a great lover of the tennis,' said her husband. 'Been watching it all day this week, haven't you, love?'

His manner towards her combined embarrassment with a kind of defensive pride.

'Yes. And I hope to see that young Yugoslav playing this afternoon. She's amazing. Supposed to be on court at two, I think.' She looked at the watch that dangled loosely from a skeletal wrist. 'Probably better start walking over there now. I'm afraid I move very slowly these days, Mr Paris.'

She was joking, but the mention of her disability served to clear the atmosphere.

'Oh, you're not that bad, love. Anyway, we've got lunch to eat first. I'm sure you'll enjoy that.'

As if on cue, Brian Tressider raised his hands, gesturing towards the interior of the marquee. 'Going through for a spot of lunch now—set us up for the excitements of the afternoon, eh?'

THERE WERE THREE round tables each seating six inside the marquee (a structure, incidentally, of greater permanence than the word usually implies). Frances, who was proving a great hit with her new friends, was whisked away to sit with them. 'Unless you'd rather sit with your husband . . . ?'

'Good heavens, no,' she replied with a sweet grin to Charles. 'We see quite enough of each other.'

He didn't quite know how to take this. Inside a normal, cohabiting marriage, such a remark would be a sign of strength, of a couple so secure in their mutual affection that they didn't need to spend every minute in each other's pockets. Given the unusual circumstances of Charles and Frances's marriage, though, the interpretation was potentially different. Did Frances really mean that their three or four meetings during the last year had been quite sufficient? Or was she just making a joke at his expense?

Charles inclined to the second view, though not with that total confidence which would make him feel secure. Frances was definitely playing games with him, but he couldn't be certain how serious those games were. She had been hurt too many times to allow the progress towards any possible reconciliation to be easy for him.

So there was Frances's table, which she seemed effortlessly to dominate; and the table towards which Brian Tressider had firmly ushered his preselected guests; and there was the third table, which was definitely lowest in the hierarchy. Charles Paris sat at the third table.

On one side of him was a young man with sleeked-back hair and a suit and tie even sharper than Charles's; on the other, a girl with carefully frizzed blonde hair, whose trim figure was enhanced by a navy leather suit that teetered between sexiness and tartiness.

It soon became apparent that they were married. The young man took Charles's hand firmly in his and announced, rather as if presenting a business card, 'Daryl Fletcher, that's my wife Shelley.'

'Hello. My name's Charles Paris.'

'We're here because it's part of Daryl's bonus.' The girl had one of those Cockney voices that sound as if the owner's just going down with a sore throat.

'Well, it's not exactly part of the bonus, just a kind of pat on the back. I got Top Salesman,' he confided to Charles.

'Oh. Oh, well done.'

'Yes. I'm North-West Area. Quite something for a North-West salesman to beat all those jammy bastards in the South.'

'I should think it is,'' Charles agreed sagely.

'Don't know they're born, half of that lot. I got Runner-up last year, but this year I really pulled out the stops.'

'Well done.'

'Means me and Shelley get a weekend for two in Paris.'

'And the car, Daryl.'

'Yeah, and the car. Get presented with that at the sales conference. I'll trade it in, mind. Just some little Fiesta. Not my sort of motor. But the money'll be handy.'

'Yeah, expect you'll just spend it on your other car.'

'All right, what if I do, Shelley? I'll see you get a bit of naughty lingerie, and all.'

This seemed to strike her as disproportionately funny.

'I got a pretty nice motor, you see,' Daryl confided to Charles. 'I don't mean the company car—no, I drive round day by day in a Ford Sierra, but I got this car back home with a bit of character.'

'Oh,' said Charles, to whom all cars had the same character.

'Cortina,' said Daryl airily.

'Oh,' said Charles, reassured. He had been afraid of being blinded by car talk, but this was all right. He had heard of the Cortina. Reliable, long-running Ford model, not out of production and a bit boring, really. But at least, he comforted himself, there's not a lot you can say about a Cortina.

Charles couldn't have been more wrong.

'It's the old Mk I,' Daryl confided.

'Oh yes?'

'Picked it up at a scrap-yard four years back. Saw its potential straight off.'

Charles couldn't conceive what possible potential a car from a scrap-yard might have.

'Basically in good nick, but I had to do a lot of body and chassis work.'

'Ah.'

'Built a full roll cage inside.'

'Did you?'

'Yeah, and then while I got the body off, I give it a four-inch chop. Pleased with the way that worked, I was. Lovely job, though I say it myself.'

He looked up for approbation, but Charles wasn't quite quick enough to replace the bewilderment in his expression with something more congratulatory.

'You do know what I mean by a "chop" don't you, Charles?'

'Er, well . . .'

'Tell you for free,' Shelly chipped in. 'It's nothing to do with a chopper!'

This again struck her as extravagantly funny.

'We are talking "custom" here,' Daryl explained generously. ' "Chop" means you take the roof down a few inches.'

'Ah. Why?'

'Well, gives you a bit of style, doesn't it?'

'Does it?'

Daryl's social training told him perhaps he ought to open the conversation out a bit. 'What do you drive then, Charles?'

A chuckle. 'Well, er, taxis, if anything.'

'You a taxi-driver?' asked Shelley.

'No.'

'What are you then?' asked Daryl.

'An actor.'

The answer struck both of them dumb. They wracked their brains for things that might be said to an actor, but nothing offered itself.

Charles filled the silence. 'What I meant was that the only cars I really travel in these days are taxis. I use the tube most of the time, but if I do go in a car, it tends to be a taxi.'

'You mean you haven't got a motor?' asked Daryl in softly awestruck tones.

'No, I haven't. Used to, when I was living with my...' He caught a glimpse of Frances entertaining her new friends at the adjacent table, 'some time back,' he concluded lamely.

'Blimey,' said Daryl quietly. 'Haven't got a motor.'
'No.'

But not for nothing had Daryl Fletcher been nominated Top Salesman. It was a salesman's job to keep talking, and he wasn't going to let anything—even a shock on the scale that he had just received—deter him from his duty.

'You know, when I took the engine on the Mk I apart, I found the cylinders were still well within specs, so what I done was...'

After about two millennia of this monologue, during which Charles, almost without noticing, consumed smoked salmon, *bœuf-en-croûte* and meringue *glace*, together with a lot of red wine, he became aware of a general movement around him.

Frances caught his eye and waved. She pointed at her watch. 'Two o'clock. Match starting on the Centre Court.'

'Oh yes, right.'

Charles started to stand up, but Frances's words had stopped Daryl in mid-description of how he'd recalibrated the gauges from an old Cortina GT. The Top Salesman rose to his feet. 'Great, I want to see this. Dishy pair of birds playing.'

Charles sank back into his chair. The risk of ending up sitting next to this cataract of Custom Car arcana was too great. 'I'll just have a cup of coffee and be right along, Frances.'

His wife shrugged and nodded. She wasn't exactly unused to Charles making his own timetable.

The marquee did not empty completely, though most of the guests went off to watch the tennis. Ken Colebourne had gone some twenty minutes earlier, gallantly escorting his fragile wife, and Brian Tressider had led his party off soon after. But a few lingered over the last of their coffee, wine or brandy.

Shelley Fletcher, Charles observed, had made no attempt to move.

'I'll go along in a bit,' she said. 'Only women on Centre Court this match.' She giggled. 'I'll wait till the hunks get out there.'

'Ah.'

'Daryl's very fond of his Cortina,' she explained, unnecessarily.

'Yes,' said Charles Paris. 'Yes, he is, isn't he?'

THIRTEEN

OUT OF THE CORNER of his eye, Charles kept catching movement on a television screen high in the corner of the marquee. White figures moved against a green background. The volume had been turned down low; applause sounded like distant sea-wash. But the picture was still distracting. He moved his chair round a little so that the screen was out of his eyeline.

This had the unintended effect of bringing him closer to Shelley. She raised her eyebrows in a quizzical, half-mocking challenge.

'I'm sorry. It's just, er, that monitor, sort of putting me off my stroke.'

'Ooh. Can't have that, can we, Charles?'

She had an engaging way of saying his name. In her husky Cockney, it came out as 'Chowss'.

'Look, I didn't mean—'

'Don't worry. I've never complained about fellers getting too close to me.'

'Ah. Ah,' said Charles. He wasn't used to this kind of heavy innuendo, certainly not from someone presumably in her mid-twenties. He adopted the traditional British method of taking the heat out of any situation. 'Lovely day, isn't it?'

She agreed that it was a lovely day. 'Nice to be down here, and all.'

'Yes. You're a Londoner, aren't you?'

'Mm. Mind you, one of the disadvantages of being married to the Top Salesman in the North-West Area is you have to live up there.' She grimaced. 'We're in Preston.'

'Is it that bad?'

'No, the people's quite friendly and that, but all my mates is really down here.' She put on a pious expression. 'Still, the little woman has to go where Hubby goes. And do whatever Hubby tells her to, and all, doesn't she?'

Shelley even managed to imbue this with a sexual overtone.

'I didn't think women thought like that nowadays. Thought you were all more liberated.'

'Oh, don't worry, Chowss, me and Daryl are a very *liberated* couple.'

He somehow didn't think they were both using the word 'liberated' in the same sense.

'And the thing is, a "liberated" couple can always find people of similar interests wherever they are. Even up in Preston. Quite a lot of "liberated" people we've met up there, you know.'

Charles nodded casually, not quite sure that he was hearing right. Shelley seemed to be saying that she and Daryl were into some kind of partner-swapping. In fact, her whole conversation could have come straight out of a soft-porn magazine. He had a sudden vision of the bookshelves in the Fletcher sitting-room—rows of Custom Car magazines, interleaved with *Penthouses* and *Escorts*.

'So are you going to be stuck up there long?' he asked uncontroversially. 'I don't know a lot about

Daryl's kind of work. Is it the sort of job where you move around a lot?'

'Yeah. Lot of salesmen do. Daryl's been with Delmoleen for a long time, working his way up, like, but now he's got Top Salesman, it's probably as far as he can go in the company. You know, he's not Sales Manager material—well, not yet, anyway—so he'll probably start looking for something else soon.'

'Something down South?'

'Hopefully, yeah.'

One of the discreet uniformed waitresses appeared beside them. 'Would you like some more wine? Madam? Sir?'

'Could probably force myself,' said Charles expansively.

Another full bottle of red wine was placed on the table between them. He gestured with it towards Shelley's empty glass.

'Why not? Neither of us got to drive. The chauffeur car's part of the day.'

'For me too.'

'Yeah. Hope you don't mind my asking, Chowss, but why are you here? Funny place for an actor to be, isn't it?'

It was a question he had been fearing, but he managed to fudge together some kind of answer about *Parton Parcel* and the filming that he had done at Stenley Curton.

'Oh yeah, how is the old place?' asked Shelley.

Charles's detective antennae started twitching. 'Why, did you ever work there?'

'Yeah, I started there as a typist straight out of school. 'Swhere I met Daryl. He was doing Midlands

Area then. We got together and...' She shrugged, 'Rest is history, innit?'

'Yes.' He took a nonchalant sip from his glass. 'I don't know if you heard, but there was a dreadful accident that day we were filming in the warehouse...?'

'Course we heard. Dayna, wasn't it?'

'That's right.'

'People been saying for a long time she was going to get her comeuppance. No one thought it'd come that way, though.'

A casual 'Oh?' proved to be quite sufficient prompting for more information.

'Well, Dayna really was a bit of a scrubber. I mean, she, like, *used* sex.'

A high moral tone had come into Shelley's voice. Clearly she regarded Dayna's behaviour as very different from her own. What was done within the confines of marriage—or, as it seemed from what she'd said, a series of marriages—was unimpeachably respectable, compared to *using* sex.

'How do you mean, exactly?'

'Well, Dayna, like, used her body to get things out of men. You know, early days she'd go out with blokes for nice meals and that. She thought the meal was OK, she'd give the bloke what he wanted. Meal not up to scratch, he didn't get nothing.'

'Not the first time that kind of transaction's happened.'

'No, right, I agree, but Dayna went on from there... you know, wanted "little presents" from blokes she went out with.'

'What kind of presents?'

'Jewellery, hi-fi, that kind of stuff.'

'Money?'

'Don't think so. Not directly. No, I think she reck-oned if it was just for money, then she might as well be a prostitute. Didn't like that idea. Oh no, our Dayna had her standards—just they was a lot lower than most other people's.'

'Ah.'

'Funny thing was, I don't think she really liked sex that much.'

'Oh?'

'Well, back in the old days, you know, before me and Daryl got married, there used to be some fairly wild parties around the place.' She looked straight into his eyes, daring him to be shocked and flinch away. 'You know, lot of couples, go to someone's house, all the bedrooms is open, play some games...maybe with forfeits—you have to take off this, take off that, girl has to go off with this bloke, bloke has to go off with that girl—you know the kind of thing I'm talking about...'

Charles nodded, as if his social life was one endless round of such parties.

'It was only fun, you know. We all had a laugh. Anyway, Dayna come along to one or two of these parties, but seemed like it wasn't her scene.'

'You don't mean she was shocked?'

'No, no, take more than that to shock Dayna. No, she joined in all right first couple of times, but then she kind of lost interest. No percentage in it for her, you see.'

'What do you mean exactly?'

'Well, like I said, she used sex to get something out of blokes. Our kind of scene, you know, where we just did it for fun . . . well, nothing in it for her.'

'Right. I see.'

Shelley giggled at some recollection. 'Coo, we used to get up to some daft stuff, though . . .'

If she started expanding too much on what they got up to, Charles was afraid he might not be able to keep up his unshocked eye contact, so he said, 'A girl who behaves like that's going to be very popular—in one sense—but she's also going to make herself pretty unpopular too, isn't she?'

'With the blokes she's dumped, you mean?'

'Yes.'

'You'd think so, wouldn't you? Funny, though, I mean a lot of the girls at Delmoleen's badmouthed her all the time . . . you know, what a slut she was and all that, but the blokes on the whole, certainly the blokes she'd been with—I mean, the ones who you'd expect to be really pissed off—I very rarely heard them say anything against her.'

'That's strange.'

'Yeah, it is actually, isn't it? Never really thought about it before, but it is strange. Like she had some hold over them or something.'

'Any idea what that hold could have been?'

Shelley shrugged. 'Why you asking all this about her, anyway?'

Charles finally broke the eye contact. 'Just interest, I suppose. You know, having been there on the day she died, and . . . well . . .'

'Mm.' Shelley stretched and looked up at the television screen. 'Looks like the ladies is coming to an end. Must go and get my seat before the hunks come on.'

'Yes,' said Charles hastily. 'Just something about one other person I met out at Stenley Curton... bloke called Trevor...'

'Trevor?' she echoed blankly.

'Drives a forklift in the warehouse.'

'Oh, *Trevor*, right.'

'He been working there a long time?'

'Well, certainly there when I started, so that's got to be five years back.'

'Yes. Was he ever involved in any of the parties you were talking about?'

'Trevor?' She let out a husky bark of laughter. 'Trevor wouldn't have fitted in to that scene at all. He'd have stuck out like a...' She chuckled throatily. 'Well, he wouldn't have stuck out at all. Ladies are not Trevor's thing.'

'Ah.' At least he'd got confirmation of Robin Pritchard's information.

'So he had nothing to do with you lot at all?'

'No, his social scene was *very* different from ours.' She paused. 'Only contact we had with him, we might borrow some stuff now and then.'

'What sort of stuff?'

'Video. Trevor was very into video. I mean, now everyone's got a camcorder, but five years ago...none of us was that well off for a start...but, you know, some of the blokes—well, and the girls, let's be fair— was quite keen to have themselves, like, re-corded...you know, while they was at it...and then play it back and get turned on all over again. You ever done that, Chowss?'

Again her mocking blue eyes were very directly fixed on his. At one level, Charles didn't take her brazenness seriously. It was a game she was playing, more for her benefit than his. At another level, though, he couldn't help being titillated by it.

He laughed what he hoped was a man-of-the-world laugh, implying infinite confident experience of every known sexual permutation.

Shelley's grin suggested that she didn't believe the implication.

'So, anyway,' he said, clearing his throat, 'you used to borrow Trevor's equipment?'

Shelley roared with laughter. 'No, like I said, that wouldn't have been any use to us at all. We borrowed his *video*.'

'Yes, yes. You knew what I meant.'

'Maybe I did, maybe I didn't.'

'Did he just lend it, like that?'

'Oh, I'm sure one of the lads bunged him a fiver. Only happened a few times. Then one of the other salesmen got a promotion and he bought his own camcorder and that was it.'

She went off into another of her giggles. 'Do you know, Daryl once rigged it up in a bedroom and filmed this couple who didn't know it was there. Then they come round to dinner couple of weeks later and he puts the cassette in the video and plays it to them. Ooh, it was funny. They were dead embarrassed. Got a really evil sense of humour, my husband,' she concluded with some pride.

That kind of practical joking didn't come under Charles's definition of 'sense of humour', but he let it pass.

'Just going back on what we were saying... you were never aware of any relationship between Trevor and Dayna, were you?'

'Relationship? Trevor and Dayna? Well, from what I've said about their interests, I can't see it, can you? She was only after rich men and he wasn't after women of any kind—doesn't sound like True Romance to me. No, if they did have any kind of relationship, you can bet your bottom dollar it was financial.'

'Hm. You say Dayna was after rich men?'

'Rich... powerful... comes to the same thing, really, dunnit? No, what Dayna wanted to do was sleep her way right to the top.'

They heard a throat clearing and turned to see Brian Tressider looking at them. Behind him was Ken Colebourne who instantly and protectively steered his Managing Director away to chat to one of their major distributors who was working his way down a brandy bottle.

But Charles had seen an unexpected look in Brian Tressider's eyes. He felt sure that the Managing Director had heard Shelley's last words.

And that they had had a particular relevance for him.

CHARLES HAD BEEN about to go and watch some tennis, but Daryl had reappeared to claim Shelley for the 'hunks' match, and the risk of accompanying them to the Centre Court was still too great. To give the Custom Car danger time to recede, Charles had another glass of wine.

Then Ken Colebourne joined him. Patricia, he announced, was quite happy watching the tennis. In fact, she was sitting with Frances and they seemed to be getting on very well. 'Still, I've never been much of a one for tennis—just knocking the ball back and forth over the net all the time, so far as I can see. Grand Prix racing, now that's the sport I like to watch.'

Charles groaned inwardly. It would be too dreadful to have jumped out of the Custom Car frying-pan straight into the Formula One fire.

But, fortunately, the Marking Director seemed to have no desire to expatiate on his hobby. Instead, he was in a mood to tell jokes and, after a few glasses of wine, Charles was prepared to indulge the mood. Even to join in it. So the two of them, fuelled by yet more wine, played that traditional pastime of mutual joke-telling which for centuries has kept men from talking about anything that matters, and given them the illusion of conviviality without any real contact.

At one point Charles did try to get the conversation on to Brian Tressider, but Ken Colebourne alertly deflected the subject. Charles was once again struck by the care with which the Marketing Director protected his boss.

And so the afternoon passed. Other Delmoleen guests drifted in and out of the marquee, tea and cakes were served at some point. Drinks were available as long as anyone wanted them, and Charles had a bonhomous sense of having chattered amiably with a great many really nice people.

They were a splendid lot, he decided, really, *really* nice people. All that nonsense that was talked about people in industry and the arts being different...

People, when you came down to it, people were people—that's what mattered. Not where they came from or what they did, but the fact that they were people. People.

He was saying this with some force to the major distributor who was working his way down a second brandy bottle and finding that, though his new friend was agreeing with him, it was still a point that needed repeating, when he became aware of a cleared throat behind him.

He turned round to see Frances. She still looked lovely in the navy suit. He told her how lovely she looked. Then, in case she hadn't got the message, he told her again.

'Yes, Charles,' she said—somewhat coldly, he thought. 'It's time we went to meet our car.'

'Oh, really? Feels like we've only just arrived.' He rose to his feet. The marquee wobbled rather endearingly around him. 'Must just have a pee.'

When he came back, Frances was thanking the Managing Director for Delmoleen's hospitality. Brenda Tressider stood by her husband's side, smiling graciously.

Charles joined in the thanks. It really had been a splendid day.

Brian Tressider was delighted he had enjoyed it.

Oh yes, it really had been a splendid day, Charles confirmed.

Brenda Tressider looked forward to seeing him on the television again soon. Were there going to be any more of that delightful *Stanislas Braid* series?

Well, no, there weren't, actually, but there was still no denying that it had been a splendid day.

Frances led him away.

He told her how lovely she looked.

'Yes, all right, Charles, you've said that.'

'Have I? Well, it's still true. I—'

'I hope you didn't make Ken Colebourne drink too much.'

'What do you mean—make him? I—'

'I was talking to his wife, Patricia. She's very worried about the amount he drinks.'

'Oh, come on, he's Marketing Director. In that kind of job, I should think the drinking goes with the territory.'

'Well, Patricia worries about it. She's very dependent on him, you know.'

What a perfect cue, thought Charles. He took his wife's arm. 'And I'm very dependent on you, you know.'

Frances firmly disengaged her arm. 'Ah, there's the car over there.'

They got in the back. 'Where to first?' asked the driver.

'Ah,' said Charles. 'Well, look, Frances, why don't we go back to your flat? Then we can have a drink, and I'll take you out for dinner and—'

'Hereford Road first, please,' said Frances. 'My companion will be getting off there.'

Charles felt he should argue, but he was really too tired. As he stretched back into the comfortable upholstery, he looked through half-closed lids at Frances. Her mouth was a tight, tense line.

Oh dear, what had he done wrong this time? He reached across to put his hand on her knee.

Frances removed it.

Well, what *had* he done wrong? It had been a splendid day. A splendid day.

It was only as he slipped into sleep that Charles realised he hadn't seen any tennis.

FOURTEEN

'I MEAN, IF YOU LIKE,' said Will Parton, 'we could do the presentation as a song-and-dance routine.'

'I think that could be terrific,' Robin Pritchard enthused. 'Really give the salesmen and their wives a bit of entertainment. Get across how exciting and up-to-the-minute the Delmoleen "Green" is going to be.'

'Look, we don't want things to get out of hand.' This voice of restraint was Ken Colebourne's. He had overall charge of the Brighton sales conference and for him the whole undertaking was already quite complicated enough. The Ambassador Hotel and Conference Suites had been long booked, but there were still many details of the programme to be arranged. Song-and-dance routines sounded like potential trouble. 'I mean, the salesmen and their wives are going to get a full professional cabaret after the Thursday evening banquet. They don't want any more of that kind of stuff. Let's keep the presentations simple.'

The Product Manager for Beverages agreed. Paul Taggart was a pugnacious little Scot, clearly suspicious of Robin Pritchard's empire-building. 'All we need to do is tell the salesmen the facts. Bring them up to date on existing products, tell them the state of play on the new products, show them the packaging, commercials if they're ready, and leave it at that.'

'But the Delmoleen "Green" is such a new concept, we want to communicate the excitement we all feel about it.'

'Robin, it is no more a new concept than Delmoleen "Surge", which I will be introducing in Brighton.'

'Of course it is, Paul. "Surge" is nothing more than a repackaging job. It's just your basic Delmoleen "Bedtime" in a different jar.'

Knocking his product was hitting a Product Manager where it hurt, and Paul Taggart responded angrily, 'It is not. The sugar content has been reduced to almost zero, the glucose content boosted, and a whole bunch of different vitamins added.'

'But it will still be perceived by the public as a simple bedtime drink.'

'No, it will not!' Paul Taggart was almost beside himself. 'That is the whole point. "Surge" is the first Delmoleen product to get away from that "bedtime" tag. It's an "any time you feel like it" beverage. "Surge" is being marketed as a health drink—not a relaxant, but a stimulant.'

'Mind you,' said Ken Colebourne judiciously, 'that is the way the basic Delmoleen drink is marketed round the world. In every other country it's sold for its stimulating and energy-giving qualities. Britain's the only place where it sells on its relaxing qualities.'

'Why is that?' Will managed to chip in curiously.

'Something to do with national character, I think,' said the Marketing Director.

Charles Paris was enjoying himself. He and Will were out at Stenley Curton to attend the first 'nuts and bolts' planning session for the Brighton sales conference. It was an evening meeting in Ken Colebourne's office. Lavish salvers of sandwiches lay on the green baize cover of the table in front of them. There were also liberal supplies of coffee and mineral water (but unfortunately nothing else).

Charles had anticipated a fairly boring session and was cheered by this entertaining conflict between the Product Managers.

'So,' Paul Taggart went on, 'the marketing of "Surge" is going to be a whole new concept for the salesmen.'

'So's the marketing of "Green".'

'But, in the long term, "Surge" is going to be the more important product. The Beverage market is much steadier. Confectionery's very volatile, always subject to changes of fashion.'

'That's nonsense,' blustered Robin Pritchard. 'And, anyway, the Delmoleen "Green" is not Confectionery. If it were, it'd attract VAT, apart from anything else, and wreak havoc with our pricing strategy. There is no way it's going to be marketed as Confectionery.'

'Well, people are hardly going to pick up a muesli bar from the Cereals display, are they?'

'The Delmoleen "Green" is a bit more than just an ordinary muesli bar, Paul. Anyway, it's not being marketed as Cereals—it's being marketed as a Snack.'

'Huh. The Snack market's even more volatile than Confectionery.'

Ken Colebourne decided it was time for mediation in the war of the Cereals and Biscuits against Beverages. 'Please, please, we've got a lot to get through. But I would like to endorse Paul's point. Given all the other entertainment the sales force're going to get, I think we want to keep our presentations at the conference as simple as we can.'

The Product Manager for Beverages smiled complacently. 'Thanks, Ken. Always the voice of sanity. What entertainment are they going to get, by the way?'

'All the usual stuff'll be laid on for the wives. Then at the Thursday banquet there's a dance band and, of course, the cabaret.'

'Who've you got?'

'Not absolutely finalised, but looks likely to be...' He mentioned the name of an American girl singer who'd been big in the charts in the early seventies.

'What, is she here doing a tour?'

'No, we're flying her over just for this.'

'That's going to cost you.'

Ken Colebourne nodded grimly. 'Got to go bigger and better than Torquay last year. Don't want any more of the salesmen thinking of moving.'

'Suppose not.'

'And then the comedy cabaret—assuming we get the contract sorted out OK—is going to be Nicky Rules.'

They were all impressed by the name. Nicky Rules was one of the country's top comedians, a television game-show host known chiefly for the viciousness with which he insulted its contestants and the glee with which the contestants lapped up his abuse.

Charles was possibly more impressed than anyone else present—not because either of the names mentioned were favourites of his, but because, being in the business, he had some idea of the kind of fees they could command. It had never occurred to him that a company like Delmoleen would be prepared to pay that sort of money just to entertain its sales force.

Robin Pritchard had been silent for the last few minutes, but not because he had conceded defeat on

the presentation of his product. He had been merely
biding his time, and now came back forcibly to the
attack.

'I still want to put across the Delmoleen "Green"
with a bit of razzmatazz. I want the salesmen to see a
presentation they're going to remember.'

'They'll remember it perfectly well if it's done
straight,' said Ken Colebourne coldly.

'No, they won't. They'll just doze off, as ever.
Look, the presentation's in the afternoon—thanks to
someone else getting the morning slot for their product...'

The Product Manager for Cereals and Biscuits
looked daggers at the Product Manager for Beverages, who grinned smugly.

'And we all know what that means—the salesmen
will have had a few too many at lunchtime and, if they
just get a straight presentation, they'll see it as a good
excuse for a kip.'

'You're out of date, Robin,' said Ken Colebourne.
'That old hard-drinking image of the salesman has
changed. They're much more responsible and ac-
countable these days.'

He had chosen the wrong line of attack. 'Out of
date?' Robin Pritchard echoed contemptuously. 'Out
of date? *You* have the nerve to call *me* out of date?'

'Well—'

'For one thing, I don't believe that salesmen ever
really change. For another, this company is going to
do nothing for its image if it keeps using presentation
methods out of the Ark.'

'Look—'

'I want the Delmoleen "Green" presented to the sales force in an exciting way, not just a talking head and slides.'

'Talking head and slides has worked perfectly well in the past.' As ever, when pressured, Ken Colebourne summoned the name of his hero as evidence. 'B.T. doesn't even bother with slides.'

'No, but Brian's a charismatic speaker. People'd listen to him, whatever the circumstances, whatever he was talking about. Other people need more help.' Robin Pritchard looked at the Marketing Director with an expression that fell little short of insolence. 'Will you be doing your usual marketing overview?'

'Yes,' said Ken Colebourne, trying not to sound defensive. 'End of the afternoon, just before B.T. speaks.'

'With slides, as ever?'

The Marketing Director's lips were tight across his teeth. 'Yes.'

'Hm. You haven't ever thought of getting someone else to do that, have you?'

'Who else? I'm Marketing Director. It seems pretty ridiculous to have anyone else talking about marketing.'

'I mean an actor.'

'What do we want bloody actors in our sales conference for?'

'Just to make the presentation look more professional.'

This gibe really got to the Marketing Director. 'Listen, I am going to do that overview, because I am the person who knows most about the subject! And if I'm not professional enough, well, that's bad luck!'

Having heard Ken's views on the subject of speaking in public, Charles was a little surprised at how vehemently the Marketing Director defended his right to do it. But then, of course, this was office politics. The argument was not primarily about who presented the marketing overview, it was just another manifestation of the protracted conflict between the two executives.

'Very well,' said Robin Pritchard lightly. 'On your own head be it, Ken…as usual. But since we have Will here, do you mind…' his voice was heavy with sarcasm, 'if I just ask him for his professional advice…?'

'No. No, go ahead.'

'OK, Will, if we could somehow persuade the dinosaurs of Delmoleen that we don't have to present "Green" to the sales force by the old sleeping-pill methods…would you have some alternative suggestions…?'

'You bet,' said the writer gleefully. 'I have thought through quite a lot of potential scenarios…'

Charles knew this was a complete lie. Will Parton had given the subject no thought at all. He was busking, but—it had to be admitted—busking quite convincingly.

'We could go up the comedy sketch path, of course—plenty of ideas there, which I'd be happy to spell out for you—but I think a more fruitful approach could be song-and-dance…you know, glitzy, bit of showbiz, get in some dancers, a choreographer *and*—' he announced, offering the spur-of-the-moment thought as if it was something he'd been mulling over for months, 'we could have all the dancers dressed in *green*.'

'This I *like*,' said Robin Pritchard, while his two colleagues looked sourly on.

'The important thing, though, Robin, is to get the right song for the presentation. I was thinking it should be something with "green" in the title.'

'An existing song, you mean?'

'Exactly.'

'But we're never actually going to find a song that's about muesli bars,' the Product Manager objected. 'Least of all *green* muesli bars.'

'No, of course we're not. But we take an existing song and we parody the lyrics.'

'Don't you get copyright problems if you do that?' asked Charles.

'Ah, you would if it was for public performance. Because it's in-house, no one's ever going to know about it. There are really no rules in the corporate world. Writers' Guild regulations don't apply. Nor do Equity, nor Musicians' Union. It's a free for all.'

'Do you have any songs in mind?' asked Robin Pritchard.

'Well, yes, there are a few obvious ones.' Will's mouth opened and closed as he wracked his brains for a single relevant title.

'*Greensleeves* . . . ?' Charles offered helpfully.

'Yes, yes, good. Or, um . . . *Mountain Greenery* . . . or . . .' The writer started to get into his stride. '*Green Tambourine* . . . *The Green Leaves of Summer* . . .'

'*Green Grow the Rashes, O!*' Charles contributed.

'Yes.'

'And that has the advantage of being out of copy-right, so there couldn't possibly be any problem.'

'No. And it could go...' Will paused, still impro-vising like mad, then started to sing, *'I'll sing you one, O!'*

Charles intoned the chorus. *'Green grow the rashes, O!'*

'What is your one, O?'

'Green grow the rashes, O!' the actor repeated, leaving the writer with the difficult bit.

A momentary light of panic crept into Will Par-ton's eye, but he recovered himself. *'One is green, completely green, and ever more shall be so!'*

'I think we really could be on to something here,' said Robin Pritchard earnestly.

'I'll sing you two, O!' Charles sang, trying to avoid Will's eye.

'Green grow the rashes, O!'

'What is your two, O?'

'Green grow the rashes, O!'

Charles suddenly realised that he had lumbered himself with the creative bit. 'Erm...erm... *Two, two the muesli bars,*

'Wrapped up all in green, ho! ho!' he pronounced with triumph.

'One is green, completely green, and ever more shall be so!' Will completed the chorus lustily.

They pressed on but Charles's control had gone. His eyes streamed and he could hardly get the words out through suppressed giggles. Will was managing bet-ter, but even his voice trembled on the edge of hys-teria.

The killer came when Will supplied the line for 'three':

'*Three—beats all ri-i-i-i-vals!*'

Charles was finished; he could only wheeze helplessly.

'This won't do,' said Robin Pritchard suddenly.

'I'm sorry,' Charles gasped. 'It just struck me as terribly—'

'No, this song—*Green Grow the Rashes, O!* It could have very unfortunate associations. It might give potential customers the idea that the Delmoleen "Green" would bring them out in a rash.'

'Oh dear, hadn't thought of that,' said Will, his voice heavy with concern. He turned sardonic eyes on his friend and the corner of his mouth twitched as he asked, 'Had you, Charles?'

'I, er...I, er...' Charles rose desperately to his feet, fighting down the hysterics. He rushed to the door of the office. 'I'm sorry,' he cried, as he sped helplessly off down the corridor. 'Asthma! Asthma!'

FIFTEEN

CHARLES REGAINED sufficient control to return to Ken Colebourne's office and nod soberly through the rest of the meeting. The office politics and power games continued, and it was interesting to see how Robin Pritchard slowly gained the ascendancy. Maybe he was demonstrating techniques he had learnt at business school, though Charles suspected that it was just the fact of his having been there that weakened his opponents. Ken Colebourne and Paul Taggart had both risen through the ranks. In the past this would have given them confidence over any mere graduate; but in the paranoid climate of a threatened recession nobody knew anything any more, and the concept of 'management training' had taken on a new mysterious potency.

The Product Manager for Cereals and Biscuits' positive gain from the meeting was the agreement to let *Parton Parcel* develop creative ideas for the presentation of the Delmoleen 'Green' at the Brighton sales conference. The Marketing Director and the Product Manager for Beverages remained uneasy, but there was no doubt that Robin Pritchard had won the round.

The meeting broke up at half-past nine, but as Charles and Will were about to leave, Ken Colebourne called the writer aside. Could they have a few words about the budget...?

Since this was clearly money talk, no doubt a bit of haggling about how much *Parton Parcel* would be paid for the additional work, Charles discreetly withdrew. Will's timetable showed that the next—and indeed the last—train back to Bedford was at ten twenty-seven, so they agreed to meet at Stenley Curton Station.

Charles emerged into a warm, moonless night. The two Product Managers had hurried off to their executive cars (and no doubt their executive homes and their executive wives). The whole Delmoleen site was very still. A few lights gleamed from the main building, presumably somewhere security officers patrolled, but Charles felt as if he was completely alone.

He looked at his watch. Leaving time to get to the station, he still had half an hour to play with. He tried to persuade himself that what he wanted to do with that half-hour was make another search for the pub that must exist in the vicinity. It wasn't difficult. The prospect of a drink was always a strong persuader to Charles Paris and, in order to look convincingly executive at that evening's meeting, he hadn't touched a drop all day.

But, in spite of the seductive image of a pub, he knew—inexorably though unwillingly—that that wasn't where he was going to go. In his suit there was something which confirmed what he had intended to do from the moment he left his bedsit that morning.

His hand closed round the small torch in his jacket pocket, and he moved cautiously towards the warehouse in which Dayna had met her death.

THE MAIN DOORS of the warehouse were firmly locked. Charles circled the building to the loading bays at the side. He climbed up on to the concrete platform the lorries backed up against, and moved along, dashing a spurt of torchlight at the bottom of each rolling shutter, but here too the padlocks were secure.

Maybe he should have secreted a crowbar about his person as well as the torch. Nobody would have noticed; the suit was voluminous enough to hide a platoon of Royal Engineers.

He sidled round to the end of the warehouse where the offices were. His eyes had by now accommodated to the meagre light and he could see quite clearly. He cast cautious looks along the alleys between other buildings, but there was no one in sight.

The door to the back office was locked, and he turned his attention to the windows. Delmoleen's warehouses didn't run to air-conditioning, so there was a possibility someone might have left a latch unfastened.

Charles felt along the frames and was rewarded by the rattle of metal on metal. A loose fanlight. He hooked his little finger under the metal ridge, then the next finger and the next. He pulled the fanlight outwards and fixed it in the open position.

He looked around again, but the darkness was unpeopled. As he reached his arm inside, the sudden thought of security alarms came to him. He withdrew his hand and ran the torchlight round the adjoining frames. There were no signs of wiring or contact-breakers.

It was still a risk, but one that he had to take. On a big enclosed site like the Delmoleen one, he told himself, most of the security devices would be on the outer perimeter fence; there were unlikely to be alarms on the individual buildings.

Whether this reasoning was correct or not, no warning bell sounded as he reached through the fanlight, firmly grasped the handle of the abutting window, raised it and pushed the pane outwards.

Breathing heavily, Charles Paris heaved himself up on to the sill and pulled his body through. It was more of an effort than he had expected, but, after some ungainly kicking, he landed in a heap on the floor. He hoped the suit hadn't got torn; still, it felt all right as he patted himself down.

He closed the window and the fanlight. Security men were bound to be patrolling at some point, and there was no need to leave a calling card for them.

Keeping the beam low, he flashed the torch round the room and then extinguished it. As expected, he was in the office where he had reported Dayna Richman's death to Brian Tressider. Oh yes, and Heather had been there too on that occasion. Charles had a sudden vision of the secretary sitting at home at that very moment, listening to her mother's continuing monologue of disparagement.

The door connecting the two offices was unlocked and he moved onwards. Through the windows ahead of him, the emptiness of the warehouse loomed.

With the interconnecting door closed, Charles Paris felt confident to leave his torch switched on. A sweep round the office revealed nothing untoward. Sheaves of invoices and dockets hung from clips on the walls. A planner chart listed staff holidays. On a calendar, gift from a haulage company, under the quaint Dick-

ensian print of dray-horses, days had been diagonally
scored through right up to the current date. Everything was neat and orderly. Heather ran a tight ship.

Charles stepped through into the body of the warehouse. The beam of his torch could not reach its ceiling, nor to the end of the long narrow aisles. His light
ran questing along past huge boxes of Delmoleen
'Bedtime', Delmoleen 'Nutty Flakes', Delmoleen 'Oat
Nuggets', Delmoleen 'Bran Bannocks', as it sought out
the aisle in which Dayna had met her death.

At the office end of the warehouse forklift trucks
stood in orderly rows, linked to the wall by their recharging cables, still, like tethered animals.

The stock had changed, but Charles counted his way
along to be certain that he had found the right place.
Then, with torch modestly lowered to illuminate only
where he took his next step, he moved down the aisle.

The setting seemed different in the softly envelop-
ing darkness, but once again there was a pile of used
pallets against the far wall. When he reached them,
Charles directed the torch across the jumble of slatted wood.

He wasn't certain what he had been looking for, but
when his beam outlined the shape of a small door
through the planks, he felt confident that he had
found it.

It was impossible to move the pallets and hold his
torch at the same time and, since there was nowhere he
could prop it to shed any useful light, he flicked the
switch off and dropped the torch into his pocket.

Charles's hands gripped at the roughly finished
wood as he tugged the first pallet away from the wall.
He tried to manoeuvre it silently, but hadn't been pre-

pared for quite how heavy it was. The sweat trickled on his temples and down the small of his back as he struggled.

Suddenly the obstruction worked itself free. Charles sprawled backwards and the pallet crashed on to the floor, just missing his legs.

The impact was grotesquely loud in the cavernous emptiness.

But no other sound followed. Apparently there was no one in the warehouse to be disturbed.

Encouraged, Charles picked himself up and felt for the outline of the next pallet. This one he jerked and worried free, tipping it out of the way with noisy abandon.

The others shifted more easily, clattering aside as more of the wall was exposed. In a matter of moments Charles had unimpeded access to the small door.

He retrieved the torch from his pocket and focused it on the metal rectangle. Battered and dusty, the door had once had a handle, but now only a small circular hole remained. Charles hooked a finger inside and pulled. The hinges creaked, as the door reluctantly moved towards him.

He shone the torch inside. The space was about two-foot square. On the facing wall was some kind of electrical equipment, old ceramic-collared sockets, thick cables snaking to brittle plastic junction boxes, a black ribbed metal box inset with a large rectangular switch.

Maybe the set-up was some kind of recharging unit for earlier designs of forklift trucks. Whatever it had been, though, it was clearly long disused. Thick dust coated the components and an uneven carpet of fluff lay on the floor.

The torchbeam flicked around the grubby walls. At first Charles could see nothing of interest, but on a second examination, he noticed something on top of the switching unit.

Black and dust-covered like the rest of the box, at first they looked like part of the structure, but now he could distinguish two flat rectangular shapes.

Charles Paris leant into the cupboard to blow away some of the dust, then gingerly reached for the top rectangle.

He sat back on his heels and trained the torch on to what he was holding.

It was a VHS cassette in a black cardboard case.

His mind just had time to register this fact, before a sudden crash of pain on the back of his neck seared fire across his eyes.

And then everything went black.

HE PROBABLY WASN'T out that long.

Maybe it was the hum of the electric motor that brought him round. Or the crunch of splintering wood.

He looked up to see two low headlights slowly approaching.

He was also aware of a lesser light source near him on the ground. It must be his torch, still switched on.

He reached for the floor, but something obstructed him. Wood. Planks of wood. He was lying on something slatted.

A pallet.

As his hand closed round the torch, he tried to lift himself up, but the movement resurrected the agonising pain at the top of his spine. He was almost blinded by it, and he knew that for the time being he was immobilised.

He pointed the pathetic beam of his torch between the oncoming headlights.

The silver maker's logo gleamed against the yellow front of a forklift truck.

Raised higher, the torchbeam cavernously shadowed the clenched face of the truck's driver.

Trevor.

And Charles Paris felt convinced that he was seeing the last thing Dayna Richman saw before she died.

SIXTEEN

HE BRACED HIMSELF for the pressure of wood against his body, but it didn't come. His fuddled senses pieced together the fact that there was nothing between him and the truck. He was not going to be crushed against the wall by a pile of pallets.

So at least, though Charles Paris's end might be the same as Dayna Richman's, the route by which he reached it was going to be different.

As the pallet jolted and shuddered beneath him, he suddenly understood what that route was to be.

Slowly he felt the wooden platform lift from the ground, and slowly, infinitely slowly, he felt it rise up through the darkness. Charles Paris had become an item of palletised stock.

And as he rose higher and higher, he remembered, with sickening clarity, the truck's 'Quick-Release' control.

Being dropped from twenty feet on a pallet would ensure that Charles Paris never gave his definitive King Lear. Even a more-than-usually-deformed Richard III looked unlikely.

In fact, the end of his acting life was in sight. And not just his acting life. If the fall didn't finish him off, a couple more pallets dropped on to his broken body should do the trick.

Or, of course, the descent of a pallet loaded with stock would leave nothing to chance.

What a way to go. Crushed by hundreds of packs of Delmoleen 'Bedtime'. The drink was marketed (at least in the British Isles) on its soporific qualities, but surely its manufacturers never intended it to impose quite so permanent a quietus.

Slowly and inexorably, Charles Paris's pallet, his proposed funeral bier, rose through the gloom.

He tried desperately to concentrate, to make his stunned mind work.

There must be something he had going for him. By the law of averages.

A quick review of his options suggested that the law of averages didn't operate in this situation.

How long had he got? Logic told him that Trevor would lift the pallet as high as possible before dropping him. And how high was that?

A little light from the headlights percolated upwards, showing the outlines of shelving on either side at the end of the aisle. The pallet was nearly level with the top shelf.

And that must be the limit of its range. The shelving was designed to use the machine's maximum reach. In a matter of seconds, Trevor would flick the 'Quick-Release'.

Charles only had one chance and it was a slim one. The platform on which he lay swayed some three or four feet from the corner of the nearest shelf. He wasn't good at heights and it wasn't a leap he would have relished in full daylight. To attempt it in the semi-darkness was probably suicidal.

On the other hand, to wait for Trevor to drop him was certainly suicidal, and if he was going to die,

Charles preferred a method that at least gave him the illusion of self-determination.

He dragged himself into a crouching position on the pallet. The pain in the back of his neck intensified, dizzying him for a second. The upright on the corner of the shelving rippled before his eyes in the uncertain light.

Still, he had no other hope. With a silent prayer to the God who got so shamefully neglected except at such moments of crisis, Charles Paris unsteadily took up the position of a starting sprinter and, kicking off with his feet, launched himself into the void.

As he did so, he felt the wood of the pallet disappear beneath him like the trapdoor under a hanging man. The impact of his body slamming and wrapping itself round the upright of the shelves compounded with the crash of the falling pallet to shake the whole warehouse.

Every part of Charles's body trembled with shock. The pain in his neck peaked, threatening unconsciousness. Life surged and flickered in him like the power of a fading generator.

But his wrenched arms still clasped the perforated steel of the shelf support.

He was still alive.

He scrabbled around with his feet, and found the reassuring solidity of the plastic-wrapped stock on the shelf below. He tensed one foot on its surface, then the other, and allowed his legs to share the weight with his strained arms.

From the darkness beneath, he heard a confused oath from Trevor, then the sound of the forklift truck being put into neutral. It could only be a moment before the operator realised what had happened.

And when he did, Charles's prospects weren't going to improve that much. The forks of the truck could all too easily knock him off his perch, or bring down any pallet of stock on which he found refuge.

Still, he'd be safer inside the shelves than dangling from their edge. Easier to lower himself to the second shelf than pull himself up to the top. Cautiously feeling his way with his feet and moving his hands from hole to hole along the metal spar, Charles slid into the gap between two loaded pallets. Holding his body up with aching arms braced on the stock, he felt gingerly with his foot for the bottom of the shelf.

At first his shoe dangled hopelessly in a void, but then his shin brushed against an upright, on which he managed to find a precarious toehold.

'You won't get away, you bastard! I'm coming to get you!'

Trevor's voice was chillingly sudden in the empty warehouse. Charles tried to squeeze himself back into the depths of the shelves, but the boxes of stock he pushed against gave way.

The webbing and plastic wrapping of that particular load must have been damaged in transit, because the cartons were loose.

Charles found himself falling forwards as the stock was dislodged.

For a second all he felt was rushing emptiness.

Then, with the impact of a car crash, the ridged metal edge of the shelf slammed into his chest, forcing the breath from his body, but at least breaking his fall—though, from the way he felt, it might have broken a few other things in the process.

But at the moment of his own crash, Charles was aware of an answering thunder from below, the clatter of falling cartons, the change of engine note of a forklift truck going into gear.

And a human cry, which was suddenly cut off.

SEVENTEEN

AT LEAST IT PROVED that Dayna Richman's death could have been accidental. One of the cartons had fallen on to the lever of the forklift truck, pushing it into gear, and the machine was once again pressing urgently against the pile of pallets.

On the other hand, for the cartons to have fallen by chance, without the agency of a human hand, remained too much of a coincidence.

But such thoughts were only allowed a fleeting passage through Charles's mind. The greater urgency was to find out what had happened to Trevor. As fast as he could, but with extreme caution and a great deal of pain, he felt his way down the end of the shelving to the warehouse floor.

As he did so, the image of Dayna's death kept flashing through his mind. It would be a tragic irony if her murderer had been trapped by the same unlikely means.

Charles leapt into the forklift's seat and pulled the lever into reverse. With a protesting grind of gears, the machine backed off. He switched off the ignition and dropped down to the floor, then peered through the confusion of pallets to the wall.

There was no sign of Trevor.

Charles reached into the debris of splintered wood and picked up his torch, which lay exactly where he had dropped it. He swung the beam round over the chaos of dented cartons.

Trevor's legs stuck out from under a mound of Delmoleen 'Oat Nuggets'.

Charles pulled the cartons away to expose the silent operator.

Trevor lay still, but he was breathing. There was a scratch on his temple from the edge of one of the boxes, and already the skin beneath was swelling into an egg. His right leg was bent awkwardly under his left.

He moaned gently as the last carton was removed. The sound wasn't a moan of agony, more the mumbling of someone asleep. Charles decided that the man was not badly injured, just temporarily knocked out.

Help must be summoned. Charles was in two minds as to whether he should be on the premises when that help came. An anonymous call to Delmoleen security and a discreet exit before they arrived might save a lot of awkward questions.

But there was something else that had to be done. With another quick check to see that Trevor could be left for a moment, Charles went across to the pallets and moved enough back to expose the small cupboard.

He opened it and swept his torchbeam round the inside.

Just one video cassette this time.

He picked it up and pushed it into one of his jacket's voluminous pockets.

Trevor's moaning was now more articulate. Words before distinguishable as consciousness returned. Charles moved across.

The operator blinked in the light of the torch. 'What the hell's going on?' Recollection returned when he saw Charles's face. 'Why, you bastard!'

He made to rise, but winced in agony as he put weight on his right leg. 'Shit! My leg—it's bloody broken!'

'I'll get help,' said Charles.

Trevor looked up, still furious through his pain. 'I wanted to kill you,' he said. 'I should have killed you!'

'Why?' asked Charles coolly.

'Because you said I killed Dayna. I can't have people going around saying that kind of thing. If that kind of rumour ever got to the police . . .'

'Well, did you kill her?'

'No, of course I bloody didn't!'

'I saw you coming into the warehouse just before she died.'

'Ah, but—'

'And don't bring up the alibi that Heather so conveniently provided for you. That's shot to pieces now.'

Trevor didn't try to argue with this.

'Incidentally, why did Heather suddenly cover up for you?'

'God knows. I was as surprised as anyone. Mind you, wasn't going to look a gift horse in the mouth. Got me out of a nasty spot and no mistake.'

'But she's not a particular friend of yours?'

Trevor shook his head. The movement reactivated the pain in his leg and he grimaced.

'I don't know,' he said when he'd recovered himself. 'Heather's devoted to Delmoleen. Well, devoted to Brian Tressider, anyway. I think she probably just saw a moment of danger to the company, and said the first thing she could think of that would stop an outside investigation.'

'And you were happy enough to go along with it?'

'Sure.' Another spasm of pain crossed Trevor's face. 'Look, I need an ambulance. Have some pity, for Christ's sake.'

'Why?' asked Charles, atypically cruel. 'You were trying to kill me. Why should I show any pity on you?'

'Because my leg bloody well hurts!'

'I'll get help in a minute. I just want you to answer a couple of questions first.'

Trevor didn't argue. 'What are they?'

'First—did you kill Dayna?'

'No, I didn't! I told you—it was an accident. I didn't intend it to work out like that.'

'But you did go into the warehouse, didn't you?'

'Yes.'

'And it was you who switched on the ignition of the forklift?'

'Yes. Yes.'

'Why?'

'Because I was bloody angry.'

'Who with?'

'You!'

'Me? What had I done?'

'You'd just got up my nose all that morning. I was angry that they thought I couldn't do my own job, that they had to bring in a bloody actor to do it for me!'

'That wasn't my fault.'

'Maybe not, but it got me livid. You didn't know a thing about forklifts.'

'No, but—'

'So I reckoned if they saw that you'd left the truck running all lunch-hour, flattening the battery, they'd realise how bloody useless you were.'

'So you switched the truck on just for that?'

'Yes.'

'But you didn't leave it in gear?'

'No, I bloody didn't!'

'Did you see Dayna come into the warehouse?'

'No. Look, all I did was I left it running... Then the cartons fell, pushed it into gear and unfortunately she was behind the pallets. It was an accident.'

Charles looked sceptical. 'Sounds pretty unlikely to me. I do know, incidentally, why Dayna was behind the pallets. She knew where you kept the videos, didn't she?'

Trevor looked even more truculent. 'So?'

'What were those videos, Trevor?'

'Oh, just some rubbish I used to sell round the factory. Porno stuff.'

'Films you'd made yourself?'

'No. No, these were things I'd copied. Could usually find a few of the blokes here who'd buy them. Anything was more exciting than their bloody wives, in most cases.'

'Did any of the videos feature Dayna?'

'No. Like I said, they was just stuff that'd been pirated.'

'But your video camera had been used for filming couples on the job,' said Charles, remembering what Shelley Fletcher had told him.

Trevor looked defiant. 'I've lent it to people. What they did with it was up to them.'

'Did Dayna ever ask you if she could borrow it?' Trevor looked up sharply at the question, so Charles pursued his intuition further. 'Did she ever ask you to film her in a sexual situation?'

'She asked. I said no.'

'So you didn't even lend her the camera?'

'Well . . . Yes, I did.'

'Why?'

'There was . . . Well, there was something she knew which . . . I didn't want anyone else to know.'

'Something about your sex-life?'

'You could say that.'

'Surely not just that you're gay?'

Trevor looked up sharply. 'How did you know? Did she tell you?'

'No, of course not. I worked it out for myself,' Charles lied. 'But surely that doesn't matter. It's no big deal these days.'

'Maybe it isn't in the bloody theatre. Place like this it's still a big deal. Have to be very careful . . . particularly if you're interested in someone else in the company . . .'

'And are you? Is there someone else in the company?'

Trevor looked almost tearful, weary, glad to confide his troubles. 'There's a boy in the Post Room. I'm pretty sure he's interested, but . . . Oh, it's difficult. That's why I was here tonight. Supposed to be meeting him here. Little bugger never showed, did he?'

'And did Dayna know about this boy? Was that the hold she had over you?'

'No, wasn't that. This little bastard's only just joined the company. No, Dayna knew about... something else.'

Charles had a sudden intuition. 'Was it something to do with minors? Under-age boys?'

Panic flared in the operator's eye. 'Did she talk to you? What did she say?'

'Nothing, nothing,' Charles soothed. 'I was just guessing.'

'Really?'

'Yes. Did Dayna say she'd got evidence against you?'

'Claimed she had. Claimed she'd photographed me outside a place... It's a gents' lavatory where...well...'

'Did you ever see the photographs?'

'No. But the place she mentioned was right, and the time she said she'd seen me.'

'Hm. And that's why you reacted against Dayna that morning when we were filming here?'

Trevor gave the smallest of nods.

'So she was blackmailing you...?' This too was confirmed. 'Just as she blackmailed other people round Delmoleen...?'

'I don't know that for sure. But I think so. I'm fairly certain that's why she wanted to borrow the camera— to set it up so she could film herself on the job.'

'With whom, though, Trevor? Who did she want to be filmed with?'

'I don't know. Really don't.'

It sounded like the truth. 'Would explain why the men she'd been with didn't criticise her too much afterwards...' Charles mused. 'She was an ambitious girl by all accounts, Dayna, wasn't she?'

'Yes. She wanted to get to the London office. Had applied for a post there just before she . . . you know, before she died.'

'Really? That's interesting. Do you know if she got the job?'

'Not certain. Think she probably did, yes.'

'Hm. I've heard people say she wanted to screw her way right to the top of the company . . .'

'Wouldn't have been out of character.'

'But you can't give me any names . . . ?'

Trevor gave a decided—but incautious—shake of his head. He winced as the pain from his leg tore through him.

'I'll call an ambulance,' said Charles. 'And, actually, I don't think I'll be around when it comes.'

'Probably just as well.'

'Another industrial accident. Likely to get as detailed an investigation as the last one.'

'I should think so.'

The atmosphere between the two men had changed. It was never going to become one of complicity or even friendship, but at least the overt hostility was gone.

'By the way,' said Charles graciously, 'I'm prepared to forget the fact that you tried to kill me.'

He got a gruff 'thank you' for that. 'I'm sorry, but I couldn't have you going round saying I'd murdered Dayna. I mean, that was bound to open up a whole can of worms about . . . you know, other things . . .'

'Don't worry. I won't make the accusation again.'

'Right. Good. So that means you know I didn't kill her.'

'Sure,' Charles agreed. 'All you did was switch on the forklift's ignition.'

And he was very close to being convinced that that really was all Trevor had done.

But he'd reserve judgement until he'd watched the video cassette that nestled in his jacket pocket.

FOR THE CALL TO SECURITY that announced an accident in the warehouse, Charles used the voice he had perfected for *Gaslight* ('Charles Paris was about as sinister as a teddy-bear with a bow round its neck'— *Leicester Mercury*). The security guard didn't sound very frightened by it either, nor particularly interested, but he said someone would be over there soon.

Charles made good his escape by the same route that he'd entered the warehouse and, to his amazement, got to Stenley Curton Station in time to join Will on the ten twenty-seven train to Bedford.

'What the hell's happened to your suit?' the writer asked.

Charles looked down. A pocket flapped, torn down one side. Two of the double-breasted buttons had gone. The fabric was scored with furrows of black dirt.

'Oh, er, I fell over,' he replied feebly.

On their journey back he told Will Parton nothing of what had happened. Nor did he mention what he was carrying in his suit's surviving pocket. This was partly because secrecy seemed essential until he'd got a few more details sorted out. And partly because he gave in to the healing sleep that his battered body cried out for.

At St Pancras, still muzzy and confused, Charles hailed a cab and gave the address of the only discreet person he could think of who owned a video.

'WHAT THE HELL'S happened to your suit?' Frances asked.

She stood in the doorway of her flat in a dressing-gown, face puffy with sleep. Someone who always hated being woken up in the middle of the night, she did at least have the restraint not to say, 'Do you know what time it is?'

'Take a long time to explain,' said Charles. 'Look, for reasons which would also take too long to explain. I need to borrow your VCR.'

Frances looked at her watch and raised her eyebrows. 'I see.'

The tape was a commercial hard-core pornographic film. The antics of the cast demonstrated a bored mechanical professionalism. There was no soundtrack, but the looks of the participants suggested a German or Scandinavian origin. None of them was recognisable from Delmoleen.

Charles looked at the screen with a mixture of cheap arousal and fascination. Incredible to think that these people belonged to the same profession as he did. Or did they? Was it necessary to have an Equity card for this kind of work? Did such performers have their own professional directory, he conjectured, like the more traditional actors' *Spotlight*? And, if they did, what kind of photographs did they put in it? And what physical characteristics did they list? It was mind-boggling.

After four or five minutes of the film, Frances said shortly, 'I'm going back to bed.'

Charles had planned an appealing, doglike look, followed by a request for permission to sleep on her sofa. There was always a chance of graduating from sofa to bed. Or of taking Frances a cup of early morning tea . . . which could always lead to a nice little restorative cuddle . . . and a nice little restorative cuddle could always lead to . . . He composed the appealing, doglike look and turned its full power on his wife.

'I'm sorry, Frances, I do have to watch this all the way through.'

'Yes, I'm sure you do, Charles,' she said drily.

'But I was wondering if I could—'

'Let yourself out when you've finished,' said Frances, and closed the door.

EIGHTEEN

'Then I awake and look around me
At the other muesli bars that surround me,
And I realise... I realise that I was only dream-
ing.
'Cause there's only one true calibre,
Full of vitamins and fibre.
Oh, there's none can touch
The green— "Green"—Del—mo—leen.'

THE SINGER STOPPED with arms outstretched and the four dancers froze in an unsteady tableau around him. The pianist folded his arms, face expressionless, mentally off-duty until next summoned to do something.

'Yes,' said Robin Pritchard, 'yes. I think that's beginning to come together.'

'We'll be running it a few more times,' Will Parton assured him. 'You know, to get it really crisp. And, of course, it'll look different when we've got the prop.'

Robin Pritchard pursed his lips. 'It's a real bugger that wasn't here for this runthrough.'

The prop to which they referred was a six-foot-long model of a Delmoleen 'Green', which was to feature prominently in the dancers' routine. The yard-broom which was deputising in the rehearsal didn't really give the same impression.

'I know,' Will concurred. 'God, I'll never use that company again. I've been on the bloody phone to them every day for the past fortnight. They swore it'd be here for today. It's just not good enough—particularly when you consider what they're charging to make the thing.'

'Well, they won't get paid, that's for certain,' said the Marketing Director with the grim satisfaction of the man who was controlling the sales conference budget.

Robin Pritchard took another critical look at the stage. 'The actual bar is going to make a big difference to the look of the thing. But I think there's no question the presentation's going to wake the sales force up. They're never going to have seen anything like that before.'

'You're certainly right there, Robin.' Ken Colebourne's expression was sardonic. He hadn't been keen on the song-and-dance idea at the outset, and nothing in its subsequent development had made him change his mind. The benefits of such presentation remained dubious, and the complications it introduced—organising accommodation for the performers, arranging the presence of a piano, having costumes and props made—were the last thing he needed at his busiest time of the year.

The strain seemed to be getting through to the Marketing Director. Charles thought he looked frazzled, and on one or two occasions when things had gone wrong in the runthrough, Ken's temper had proved to be very short. Still, putting on a major sales conference must be a stressful business. Or then again, Ken Colebourne might have problems at home. Perhaps Patricia's health was deteriorating further. One could never really know the pressures inside a marriage like that.

'I wonder if you want me to make it a bit more Tom Jones-like?' the singer asked.

He was an identikit club singer, spreading to fat, with hair dyed black to give him an ersatz Mediterranean look. Though currently in pastel golfer's leisurewear, he was the kind of performer, Charles felt sure, whose stage suit was a shiny midnight-blue tuxedo worn over ruffled shirt and corset-like cummerbund.

'How do you mean exactly?' asked Will.

'Well, I could do a bit more... you know, gyration of the hips. Make it more obviously Tom Jones. I mean, I'm doing his voice, so a lot of them are going to get it all right, but we want them all to recognise that it is Tom Jones I'm doing, don't we?'

'Most of them won't even know who Tom Jones *is*,' muttered Daryl Fletcher truculently. He had been dragged down to the conference hall because Ken Colebourne insisted that they should rehearse the presentation of his car, and Daryl really didn't think his presence was necessary. He'd rather have been up in the Panorama Bar on the eighth floor, knocking back a few drinks and lording it over the other salesmen whose annual figures hadn't been as good as his.

Actually, Charles agreed with Daryl's reservation. Although he had shared Will's excitement when they decided to parody *The Green, Green Grass of Home* for the launch, and shared the hilarity with which they had adapted the lyrics, he had always had a sneaking suspicion there was something wrong about the choice. A 1966 hit for a singer who'd since virtually given up the British scene for the lucrative American cabaret circuit was not calculated to strike many chords in the hearts of salesmen in their twenties.

'No, I think what you're doing's probably enough, erm...' Will Parton had completely forgotten the singer's name, 'love,' he concluded safely.

Actually, the 'love' was a bit more than just a cop-out. Now Will was directing, he had become frightfully showbiz. It must have been all those patient years of being a television writer—agreeing with directors' increasingly illogical suggestions, meekly rewriting and rewriting until his original concepts vanished in a welter of words—that made him so relish the role. Here, in the unobserved environment of the Brighton Ambassador Hotel and Conference Suite, he could indulge his show business fantasies and gain a private, but sweet, revenge on every director he had ever worked with.

'Now have you tried on the cozzies yet?' he continued, directorially bossy.

'When?' asked one of the bored female dancers. 'We was called for two o'clock, we've been here since two o'clock. It's now eight o'clock. When are we supposed to have had time to try on costumes, eh?'

They had been kept busy all that time. There were two men and two women, though the one who rather grandly designated himself 'Dance Captain' kept referring to them as 'boys and girls'. He had kept them at it, learning the very basic choreography of their number and the necessary manipulations of the yard-broom, on the stage when it was free and at the back of the hall when it wasn't. The rehearsal they had just done had been the first full one, with music and singer.

Clearly more work was needed, but Ken Colebourne
kept looking anxiously at his watch. They were over-
running their scheduled time, and there was still a lot
to be run through.

'We got to move this on, Will,' he said.

'Yes, of course. Time for one more run of the
song?'

'No.'

'Oh, come on, it's not up to standard yet,' Robin
Pritchard protested.

'That is your problem, not mine,' said Ken Colebourne, with a degree of satisfaction. 'If you'd kept
the presentation simple, we'd be finished by now.'

The Product Manager for Biscuits and Cereals ar-
gued, but for once he didn't get his own way. Despite
the stresses of what he was doing, Ken Colebourne had
great experience of organising sales conferences, and
there was no doubt that he was in charge. Robin Pritchard accepted defeat, and went off with his grum-
bling singer and dancers for a dress parade. The singer
was to wear a green tuxedo, the 'boys' green waistcoats and trousers, and the 'girls' green catsuits.

'OK. Next I want to run my marketing overview sequence,' said Ken. Then he noticed someone hovering at the back of the hall, trying to attract his
attention. 'Yes, Heather, what is it?'

Charles turned to see the secretary from the warehouse step forward. He was not surprised to see her.
Apparently the two days of the sales conference was a
kind of bonus granted the more senior Delmoleen office administration staff. According to the nudging
information of Daryl Fletcher, most of them used this
as an annual license for a bit of extramarital hanky-

panky. As Heather Routledge coughed diffidently before speaking, Charles could not somehow imagine her to be involved in any such goings on.

'There was a message for you, Ken. Could you ring Nicky Rules?'

'Oh, God, he's not going to cancel on me, is he?' The Marketing Director had so much on his plate at that moment that the thought of having to find a new cabaret for the following night's banquet was more than he could contemplate.

'No, it's all right. Just a couple of things he wants to check about the company.'

'Oh, all right. I'll ring him when we're through here. Thanks, Heather.'

She walked awkwardly back out of the hall. She wasn't actually ungainly, Charles decided, just lacking in confidence. Her movements had the self-defeating clumsiness of someone desperately unwilling to draw attention to herself.

'I don't know,' said Ken to Will. 'That Nicky Rules does go on. Prides himself on tailoring his material to his audience. Likes to make in-jokes about people in the company. So he's on the blower to me about three times a day. And I gather he's been talking to other management people too. Suppose I should be grateful that he bothers, but, God, it all takes time.'

He moved towards the stage. 'Right, I'll do my presentation. Just to check that the script's coming up right and the slides are in the right order.'

'Oh, look, when do we get to my bit?' Daryl Fletcher complained, seeing more valuable drinking time slip away.

'My piece runs straight into the video that introduces B.T.—that's all clips of him from television...on *The Money Programme*, interviewed at the CBI conference, in that environmental series, all that stuff. Once we've played the video, B.T. comes on, does his talk and finishes up by presenting you with the car.'

'Well, is he going to be here for the rehearsal?'

'No, he's hosting a reception upstairs.'

'Look, if Brian Tressider isn't bloody here, I don't see why I should have to bloody—'

'Daryl!'

Ken Colebourne's authority was unmistakable. The Top Salesman subsided into ungracious silence.

'Right, I'll make this as quick as I can.' The Marketing Director strode on to the stage and spoke into a microphone. 'Are you ready in the box? Marketing Director's Report—OK? Got the script lined up?'

'Yes. It's there on the autocue,' a disembodied voice replied over the talkback. 'Who's operating the slides?'

'I am.' Ken Colebourne picked up the control from a lectern. 'That way there's no chance of them getting out of synch.'

He launched into his spiel. He was a workmanlike but not a charismatic speaker, reading with level intonation from the autocue on the transparent lectern in front of him, and punching up the relevant slides at the relevant moments. Packshots of products appeared on the screen behind him, graphs of sales figures, pie-charts of market shares. It was all competent, and rather dull.

Charles felt bored. He had done his bit. Will had fulfilled his promise to find something in the sales conference for Charles Paris. Early thoughts of including him in the Delmoleen 'Green' presentation had fortunately been abandoned. Although Charles had served his time in musicals, singing was not one of his strong points, and his dancing had cut a swathe of despair through battalions of choreographers. Indeed, the *Walton and Weybridge Informer* had once reviewed his performance in *My Fair Lady* in the following uncharitable terms: 'Charles Paris's Professor Higgins is the best argument I've ever seen against turning *Pygmalion* into a musical.'

But a convenient non-singing, non-dancing role in the Delmoleen sales conference had been found for him. The Product Manager for Confectionery, though very effective at his job, suffered from a mild stutter which was exacerbated by the strains of public speaking, so Charles had been delegated to present the current state of the confectionery market. It was not the most complex role he had ever been faced with, but his reading of it in rehearsal had apparently satisfied the Delmoleen audience.

Even though he'd done his bit, Charles didn't really feel he could leave the conference hall. He was also there in his *Parton Parcel* capacity, and was even wearing his suit to prove it. (The suit, incidentally, had been cleaned and had had its pocket invisibly mended. The effect of these ministrations had been to rob it of its designer shapelessness. Now it just looked shapeless.) So he thought he'd have to sit out the full term of the rehearsal, although he could feel painfully the allure of bars and receptions in the hotel above him.

Once again, as in all the Delmoleen 'shirtsleeve' sessions, lavish salvers of sandwiches had been produced. And, once again—to Charles's considerable disappointment—no liquid stronger than mineral water.

He sneaked a look at his watch. Half-past eight now. Oh, he really could murder a large Bell's.

He half-heard the drone of Ken Colebourne's presentation.

'And we still stand by the principles which made the company successful when it started. We take pride in those principles. Everyone who works for Delmoleen knows that all our products are made by the most modern manufacturing methods...'

Ken Colebourne clicked the control in his hand. A slide of a factory interior full of gleaming machinery, tended by immaculate workers in white overalls, was shown.

'They know the same high quality Delmoleen goods are sold all over the world...'

On the screen, in front of a rusty corrugated iron hut, next to a broken-down tractor, two grinning Caribbean children held up a pack of Delmoleen 'Bran Bannocks'.

'They know what the public think of Delmoleen. They know that the public trust the guarantee of hygiene that only comes from Delmoleen—and not from other companies I could mention.'

The screen filled with newspaper headlines about a scandal from earlier in the year which had crippled one of Delmoleen's main rivals. '"THEY'RE RUBBISH! I'LL NEVER TOUCH ANYTHING THEY MANUFACTURE AGAIN!" SAYS BOTULISM BOY'S HEARTBREAK

MOTHER.' (This slide was guaranteed to produce a big laugh from its salesmen audience.)

'And they know that Delmoleen goods are sold at a price that's more than competitive . . .'

Another click of the control produced a slide showing a dull semicircle of rival bedtime drinks, all marked with their inflated prices. In the foreground, brightly lit, stood a carton of Delmoleen 'Bedtime', almost eclipsed by a huge price label of '98p'.

'So they begin to understand what being a part of the Delmoleen family is really worth. And, in these environmentally-conscious times, they know that Delmoleen products are only made from the freshest of organically-grown natural ingredients . . .'

A still life of expensively photographed vegetables appeared on the screen.

'Yes, Delmoleen cares. Delmoleen is like a family. And I want to show you what sort of people are part of the Delmoleen family . . .'

A slide appeared of half a dozen workers grouped under the arch of the company logo. There were a couple in shining blue overalls, a couple in white, a man and a woman in business suits. They were carefully selected to show a mix of ages and ethnic origins. All wore gleaming smiles.

'Next,' said Ken Colebourne, 'you're going to be addressed by the man who keeps that family atmosphere and that family success going—our Managing Director, Brian Tressider. But, first, let's see some of the occasions when he's been in the public eye during the last year. And, seeing this, you'll ask yourself how he manages to fit everything in to just twenty-four hours a day. He seems to be at it all the time!'

This was the cue for the video. The slide of smiling workers disappeared, and instantly the screen filled.

But what filled it was not a compilation of Brian Tressider's media appearances during the previous year.

Instead, two naked bodies thrashed against each other in the steamy heat of a sexual encounter.

Daryl, whose expression suggested he knew of the substitution, sniggered, and Charles, suddenly seeing the aptness of Ken Colebourne's introductory words, could not hold back his own laughter. Will Parton also started giggling.

The Marketing Director was looking out front, puzzled, and it took him a moment to turn and face the source of their amusement.

When he did, his reaction was instantaneous and furious. 'Where the hell did you get that from? Stop it!' he screamed into the microphone. 'Stop it! We mustn't see any more! B.T.'d go mad if he knew about it! He thinks it's been destroyed. Stop that bloody tape!'

The unseen operator at the back of the hall, either from genuine incompetence or because he was enjoying the joke, took a while to obey this command, which gave the audience time to see more of the action.

And what Charles saw told him that this was just another commercial pornographic tape. The participants had nothing to do with Delmoleen. Certainly the man was totally unlike Brian Tressider.

What was interesting, though, was not the tape itself, but Ken Colebourne's reaction to it. Or rather his over-reaction.

He had panicked completely. And, though he could soon recognise that his Managing Director didn't feature, what Ken had said suggested that it wouldn't have surprised him to see Brian Tressider in such compromising circumstances.

NINETEEN

'NAH, IT WAS JUST A LAUGH,' said Shelley. 'Daryl's always doing stuff like that. His sense of humour's bleeding mental.'

'So he wasn't making any point by getting the video shown?'

'No, Chowss, he doesn't work like that. Daryl was just miffed that he had to go and sit through hours of rehearsal when all he was going to have to do was say "Thank you very much for my car." So he thought "What can I do to liven things up a bit? I know, bung the bloke in the control box a fiver—get him to show a smutty video." That's how his mind works. It's only a joke—that's Daryl all over.'

She looked affectionately across the bar to where her husband was drinking and swapping either scatological jokes or custom car minutiae with a bunch of fellow salesmen.

Charles was inclined to believe her. It would have been in character for Daryl to stage that kind of meaningless prank. And there was no reason to believe that the Top Salesman had any suspicions about Dayna Richman's death, so he really had no other motive for doing it.

For Charles, on the other hand, the video—or rather Ken Colebourne's reaction to it—had triggered an avalanche of new thoughts.

The Marketing Director's first response, before he saw what was actually being shown, was the one that mattered. He had panicked, thinking what was on the screen was not a commercial product, but a secretly-filmed video of a man and a woman making love.

Charles only knew of one person in the Delmoleen set-up who had ever been into that kind of stuff. Dayna.

She had tried to persuade Trevor to film her with a sexual partner, and blackmail seemed to be a speciality of hers. Even though the forklift operator said he'd refused her request, it was quite possible that she'd found someone else more ready to co-operate. Or indeed she could have set up the apparatus herself. It wouldn't have been a problem; camcorders were getting easier to use all the time.

Assuming then that such a blackmailing tape existed—and Ken Colebourne's reaction suggested he knew it did—the question arose as to who was Dayna's co-star.

And Charles didn't reckon he had to look far for the answer. Dayna Richman had made no secret of her intention to screw her way to the top. She had confronted Brian Tressider in an unequivocally sexy way in the warehouse on the day she died. And, what was more, he had been on the premises at the time when her 'accident' happened. The scandal her disclosure of their relationship might cause to a man in his position was quite sufficient motive for murder.

All the evidence suddenly seemed to be pointing in the same direction.

'Well, all that looks bloody boring.'

Shelley's words brought him back to the present. She was looking disparagingly at a printed sheet of paper.

'What's that?'

'"The Wives' Programme."' Her voice was heavy with irony. 'Always at these conferences they set up some exciting things for the little ladies to do while the men are stuck in meetings.' She held the paper out. 'Look—"Visit to the Royal Pavilion and tour of its kitchens; Shopping in the Lanes; Lunch; then a Tour of a Local Winery, followed by Cream Tea"... Well, stuff that for a game of soldiers!'

'Doesn't appeal?'

'No, bleeding boring. Got all the other wives to cope with, apart from anything else. Dreary load of old bags most of them are. And dear Brenda Tressider leading us on, like some bleeding Chief Guide or Brown Owl. Won't catch me doing any of that, I can tell you.'

'So how're you proposing to spend tomorrow?' asked Charles.

Shelley grinned a rather mischievous little grin. 'Thought I might look for some entertainment here.'

'Here? What, at the conference, you mean?'

'Nah. Upstairs in my room is what I mean. Do I make myself clear?'

She certainly did. Charles was once again struck by how very attractive she was. Shelley Fletcher had that overt sexiness which can always override masculine better judgement.

She chuckled throatily. 'Might you be free then during the day tomorrow, Chowss?'

He was hooked instantly. 'Well, yes. I've got to do the Confectionery presentation, but that's first thing in the morning, so, say, after eleven...yes, I am pretty well free.'

She turned the full beam of her blue eyes on to his. 'Good. Good.'

'Good,' Charles echoed.

''Cause Daryl and some of the lads'll be able to sneak out from the odd session, I'm sure.'

'Oh?' said Charles.

'And some of the secretaries, and some of the wives'n' all—there are a few who swing a bit and wouldn't be that keen on the Royal Pavilion, if someone suggested the right alternative...'

'Ah.'

'No, I think we could have a nice time tomorrow, Chowss,' she purred.

'Tomorrow. Oh, *tomorrow*. Oh, Damn,' he said, preparing to lie. 'I've suddenly remembered Will Parton, my partner in this business, is insisting that I should sit in on as many of the conference sessions as possible tomorrow.'

He'd had no alternative. He knew it was a hopelessly old-fashioned reaction, but—much though he would have relished an individual encounter with Shelley Fletcher—Charles Paris had never been able to come to terms with the idea of sex as a community activity.

PERHAPS because his day's drinking had started so late, Charles did find he was rather making up for lost time. Or it may have been the company. The Delmoleen salesmen and their wives seemed determined to enjoy their employers' hospitality to the full, and round of drinks followed round with astonishing fluency.

It was only when he crossed the hotel's reception area to find a Gents and felt a blast of cold air from outside, that Charles realised how drunk he was. Must slow down, he thought. Mustn't cock up the Confectionery presentation in the morning. A speech delivered by someone with a really bad hangover wouldn't be much improvement over one delivered by a man with a stutter.

'Excuse me,' asked a voice from the reception desk, 'are you Mr Paris?'

'What? Oh. Yes.'

'There was a telephone message for you. Could you ring Mr Skellern as soon as possible, please?'

'Right. Thanks,' said Charles, as he stumbled on towards the Gents.

Very unusual, he thought as he peed copiously, for Maurice to be ringing him. But he didn't have the warm feeling that an actor traditionally gets from a message to ring his agent. His first thought was not that the National Theatre had suddenly decided they wanted him to do his Hamlet. Nor that Hollywood had finally made a decision in his favour about who the new James Bond was to be. No, his first thought was that Maurice had somehow found out that his client was working without telling him.

Yes, Charles would return the call. But 'as soon as possible' might not be very soon.

Thinking of phone calls, he must ring Frances too. Been a bit unfortunate, their last encounter. Well, their last two encounters, come to that. The day at Wimbledon hadn't been a major social triumph. No, little bit of minor fence-mending might be needed there. Must ring Frances and sort things out with her. Soon.

But not tonight. Always better to be sober when attempting reconciliation with his wife.

One more drink, he thought as he re-entered the bar. Just one, then I'll stop. Need a clear head for the morning.

But with the number of such good intentions he had formulated in his life, Charles could have laid out a five-lane motorway to hell. The one drink became four, and those escalated into Room Service bottles of whisky in his bedroom with Will Parton and a bunch of salesmen whose precise names Charles couldn't recall but whom he knew all to be very good chaps.

Rendered incautious by alcohol, Charles and Will started saying what they really thought about the corporate world. All the giggling they had been carefully holding in for the last weeks burst out, and Charles found the salesmen an easy and indulgent audience for his impression of Robin Pritchard.

'It's so *big*,' he was saying. 'I mean, *big* on a *global* scale. You know, we're talking *cosmic outreach* here. I mean, on a scale of one to ten, the concept scores a cool hundred. We are not talking ordinary muesli bar here, we are talking *galactic* muesli bar.'

The salesmen roared their appreciation, encouraging him to continue.

'And the revolutionary thing about this new muesli bar—I mean, the, like *globally*, *cosmically* different element in its concept—is that the new Delmoleen "Green" tastes exactly like a pan-scourer!'

The salesmen loved this too. They roared again. In fact, the hilarity was so general and so raucous that none of them heard the door open.

'Could you keep the noise down, please!'

In the doorway, with a face like a glacier, stood Brenda Tressider.

TWENTY

EVERYONE WAS suddenly sober. With mumbled apologies and subdued good nights, Charles's guests filed past Brenda back to their own rooms. When they had all gone, she shrugged apologetically. 'I'm sorry. Ken Colebourne's got the suite above you here. I don't want him disturbed. His wife Patricia's not at all well.'

'No, *I*'m sorry,' said Charles. 'Just all got a bit out of hand.'

'Yes.' He had expected her to turn on her heels and leave immediately. To his surprise, she lingered, as if undecided.

He gestured to the debris of abandoned glasses. 'Can I offer you a drink or something?'

She came forward determinedly and sat down in an armchair. 'Do you have any mineral water?'

'Tap.'

'All right.'

He took a glass into the bathroom, swilled it out and filled it. Brenda Tressider thanked him as profusely as if he had handed her a glass of Dom Perignon. As ever, her manners were impeccable. And, as ever, she was impeccably costumed—on this occasion in the little black dress she had worn for the evening's reception.

Instinctively, he found himself draining the remains of a whisky bottle into his own glass before sitting on the edge of the bed opposite her. But his head felt clear, his mind sharp.

'You shouldn't do that kind of thing when the salesmen are around,' Brenda Tressider announced.

'What kind of thing?'

'Knocking the product. Knocking Delmoleen.'

'Oh, it was just a joke. It was—'

She overrode him. 'You still shouldn't do it. It's hard enough to motivate the sales force at the best of times. If they start thinking it's all right to make fun of the company, they stop believing in it.'

'I'm sorry.'

'It's easy enough for you. You come in from outside, you have no loyalty to Delmoleen, no doubt the whole business is just a laugh for you—'

'No, I wouldn't say—'

'For the people in the company, it's their lives, it's their jobs. It's important that they believe in it...'

Charles Paris was properly chastened. He nodded abjectly. 'I'm sorry.'

To his surprise, he saw the shadow of a smile on Brenda Tressider's lips, '...even in the teeth of the evidence.'

'What do you mean?'

'I mean that faith in Delmoleen is like any other faith. You have to limit knowledge for it to grow.' She responded to his quizzical expression. 'If you start actually analysing the company, analysing what it's doing, how it works, all that...well, you couldn't possibly sustain your belief in it. So you have to close your mind to the detail, and just hold on to the faith for its own sake.'

'And exercises like this sales conference take place to reinforce that faith?'

'Exactly. Just like a Revivalist Meeting. All this tub-thumping, all this talk of "the Delmoleen family", the video you've been involved in . . . it's all there for the same purpose. You may not actually be able to make the sales force believe in the company, but at least you can get them to suspend their disbelief in it.'

Charles hadn't expected her to be the kind of woman who quoted Coleridge. 'And impersonations of Robin Pritchard make it more difficult for the disbelief to be suspended?'

'Yes, they do . . .' She smiled before the compliment, 'However accurate those impersonations may be.'

'And what about you, Mrs Tressider? Do you believe in Delmoleen?'

'It's my job to believe in Delmoleen,' she replied drily. 'Or my job to believe in Brian, which comes to the same thing.'

'And do you ever have problems suspending *your* disbelief?'

She sighed. 'It doesn't really matter whether I do or don't. I have a function to perform in the company, just as he does. I have to ensure that Brian can operate at his maximum efficiency, I have to see that the home runs smoothly, I have to be on hand for business entertaining . . .'

'You have to make small talk and sound interested in the conversation of all kinds of boring people . . . ?'

'I didn't say that, Mr Paris. You did.'

'You're very discreet.'

'Something which you, it appears, could not be accused of.'

'No. I'm sorry. You've had much more practice at it than I have.'

'That is certainly true.'

'So... your life must run on a pretty tight timetable?'

'That is also true.'

'It must sometimes have been hard reconciling the demands of your home and the company.'

'Sometimes.'

'Particularly when you had young children around.'

'Brian and I have no children, so that problem never arose.'

'Ah.' He wasn't sure whether or not he should say he was sorry. There had been no self-pity or other discernible emotion in her words.

'No, I have great respect for women who manage the demands of a family as well as everything else.'

'So you see your role in life exclusively as looking after Brian?'

'Yes.'

'There are some people nowadays...' he began cautiously '—some women, certainly—who would think that was rather an old-fashioned view of a wife's role.'

'They can think what they like. I have no doubt at all that I work extremely hard to fulfil a very necessary function. I don't see myself as subservient to Brian. I think my contribution to the success of Delmoleen is quite equal to his—and, if you asked him, I think Brian would say the same.'

'Ah. Well. Good.' Charles took a swig of his whisky. He was playing for time. He needed to move the conversation on to a more controversial tack, and he wasn't certain of the most tactful way to do it. In fact, he rather wondered whether there was a tactful way of accusing someone's husband of murder.

'Mrs Tressider...' he hazarded, 'presumably someone in Brian's position has to be very careful not to become involved in any scandal...?'

'Naturally. Any public figure is aware of that danger. The press these days are all too ready to pillory people.'

'Yes...' He hesitated again. 'In a set-up that has as many employees as Delmoleen, you're inevitably going to get a few bad apples, people who might bring the company name into disrepute...'

'You run that risk, yes, obviously. But you try to minimise it by careful recruitment and quick dismissal when you realise you've made a mistake.'

Charles nodded, wondering if Brenda Tressider's professional poise ever broke down. She was so in control, he felt an unworthy desire to see her crack just once, to see the vulnerable female beneath the carapace. But maybe there wasn't one.

He decided he'd have to cast caution to the winds and plunge in. 'Mrs Tressider, you remember the young girl who was killed in the warehouse accident the day we were making the video there...?'

Her filing system was as infallible as ever. 'Of course. Dayna Richman.'

'I've heard rumours about the place that she was into a bit of blackmail...'

'Oh?' The monosyllable was almost without intonation.

'Rumours that she used sex to blackmail men in the
company... Rumours in fact that video tapes existed
of her with senior members—or at least a video tape
of her with a senior member—of the Delmoleen management...'

'Ah.' This monosyllable contained more. In fact, it
contained a lot—an acceptance of a revised situation
and the need for a new approach to cope with that situation. But still Brenda Tressider showed no untoward emotion. 'Brian had hoped that no one else knew
about that. He thought the information had been
contained. It will distress him considerably to know
that it's common gossip round the company.'

'It's certainly not that,' Charles hastened to assure
her. 'I had to make fairly detailed investigations to
find out about it.'

'Good. So are you the only person who knows
about the existence of the tape?'

'Possibly, yes. Except for the other participant, I
assume. It seems reasonable to suppose that Dayna
had told him about the tape, had asked for money in
exchange for it...'

'Yes. She had,' Brenda confirmed. 'And now you're
doing the same, are you? How much do you want?'

'No, it's not that.'

'Don't play games with me, Mr Paris. You can't
have any other reason for raising the matter. Come on,
tell me your price. I'm sure Brian won't have any dif-
ficulty raising the money—so long as you're not asking something ridiculous.'

'Mrs Tressider, I am not asking for money—honestly I'm not.'

'Then why are you talking about the tape?'

'Because I'm trying to find out what happened to Dayna Richman.'

'We know what happened to Dayna Richman. She was killed in an accident in the warehouse at Stenley Curton.'

She said this in such an unarguable, matter-of-fact way that Charles was convinced she really did have no suspicions about the death. Though Brenda Tressider would apparently accept with equanimity her husband's infidelity, the idea that his offence might be more serious did not enter her head.

'Listen, Mrs Tressider, the timing of Dayna's death was, to say the least, coincidental.'

'What do you mean?'

'There are various traditional methods of stopping the demands of blackmailers. One is by paying them off—though the victim can never under those circumstances feel quite secure that the demands won't recur...'

'They won't recur if the incriminating evidence has been handed over in exchange for the money.'

Charles grimaced. 'Depends. What we're talking about here is a video tape. Very easy thing to copy these days, Mrs Tressider.'

'Yes. I hadn't thought of that.'

'Anyway, as I was about to say, there is another, more permanent, way of putting an end to the demands of a blackmailer.'

The idea was so alien to her that, for a moment, she did not understand him. But, as light dawned, he was

rewarded by Brenda Tressider's first uncontrolled reaction—one of shock. 'Are you suggesting that the girl
was murdered?'

'Yes.'

She quickly had command of herself again. 'That's
ridiculous.'

'I don't think so. Look, the girl had somehow arranged to video herself in bed with him, she lets him
know she's got the tape, she names her price. But he
doesn't feel certain that he'll be buying her permanent silence by paying the demand...so he decides on
a more reliable method of keeping her quiet.'

'But I just can't believe it of him. He's the gentlest
of men. I mean, I know he has a rough diamond exterior, but, deep down, he wouldn't hurt a fly. You
only have to see him with—'

'I'm afraid, Mrs Tressider, that maybe you don't
know your husband as well as you think you do.'

He had been hoping for more reaction, and he was
certainly rewarded this time. Her face became a mask
of amazement. 'My *husband*?'

'Yes, Mrs Tressider. Your husband, Brian.'

'You mean you thought the video was of Dayna
Richman and *Brian*?'

'Yes.'

She shook her head in disbelief. 'Well, I can assure
you it wasn't, Mr Paris.'

'You can't be so sure. I know it's sometimes hard
for a wife to imagine that her husband—'

'Mr Paris, Brian and I have no sex-life at all. We
haven't had for nearly thirty years. That's why we
haven't got any children.'

'I'm sorry to have to say this, but it is possible that, flattered by the attentions of a younger woman—'

'No, Mr Paris!' She was almost shouting now. 'It is not possible. Will you please give me the credit for knowing my own husband's medical condition? Brian was involved in a car crash when he was twenty-five, just after we were married. He escaped, fortunately, with what they described as 'minor injuries'. *Un*fortunately, one of those 'minor injuries' put paid to our sex-life. And not just *our* sex-life—Brian's sex-life with anyone else. So, Mr Paris, you can forget your fantasies of my husband frolicking between the sheets with Dayna Richman. I am sorry to say that, though he's very powerful in every other department of his life, down there nothing works at all!'

This time he got all the reaction he had hoped for. Tears poured down Brenda Tressider's face, furrowing through the expertly-applied make-up.

Charles Paris felt a complete heel.

OF COURSE she wouldn't give him any more information. She left his room as soon as she'd recovered from this unseemly breakdown of control. And she recovered very quickly. She'd had a lot of practice at that sort of thing through the long charade of her marriage.

But she'd told Charles enough. If it wasn't Brian Tressider whom Dayna had been blackmailing, there was only one other person it could be.

TWENTY-ONE

In spite of the volume of whisky he'd consumed, Charles only slept fleetingly. He didn't feel drunk, but his mind was very full. If he did doze off for a few minutes, he would quickly reawaken with a new link of logic connecting in his brain.

It all fell into place now. Most of the sequence of solution had been complete when he had cast Brian Tressider as murderer. With a new actor in that role, it all worked even better. The logic was tighter, the conclusion more secure.

He woke for the last time around quarter to six. His head didn't quite ache, but felt scraped and empty with tiredness. He went down to breakfast early, thinking his quarry might do the same, but was out of luck.

Never mind. Time enough. The murderer didn't know that suspicions were homing in on him. It was unlikely that Brenda Tressider would have tipped him off, so Charles need not feel in any danger. He could bide his time, and make the confrontation whenever a convenient moment arose.

Charles Paris ate a large breakfast and did his Confectionery presentation very professionally. Modern conference technology actually made it difficult to do otherwise. The script was on a roller, its speed controlled by an operator in the glass box at the back of the hall. This was relayed to a television monitor concealed on the floor behind the lectern, whence it was projected up on to an angled screen of special glass, where the words were visible to the reader but transparent to the audience. And for the Confectionery presentation, unlike Ken Colebourne's, the slides were also controlled from the box.

So, so long as the speaker had had a runthrough and knew the contents of his text, it was pretty hard to go wrong. Particularly if, like Charles Paris, that speaker had spent much of his life reading scripts.

This conference was the first time he had used such apparatus and, seeing how easy the system was, Charles vowed in future to be even more sceptical of the oratory of politicians. It was now possible for any fool to look sincere or appear to struggle for the apposite *bon mot* with a script rolling comfortingly in front of him, unseen by his audience.

After Confectionery, there was a coffee-break and then Paul Taggart did Beverages. His approach was totally businesslike and functional; he supported his argument with slides and did not allow the presentation to be sullied by humour. The eyes of the massed rows of salesmen in floppy suits and Post-Surrealist ties glazed over in the final extended agony of last night's hangover before the blessed resuscitation of a lunchtime drink.

There was no sign of Daryl Fletcher, and a few of the other seats were empty. Charles wondered idly how many Shelley had recruited to join in her day's entertainment.

He also wondered how the glazed salesmen would react to the more upbeat presentation of the Delmoleen 'Green', which was to begin the afternoon's proceedings.

Will Parton was optimistic as they joined the rush for the bars the minute Paul Taggart had delivered his final statistic. 'Going to be great, Charles,' he enthused. 'After that lot, the Tom Jones routine'll really knock 'em dead.'

Charles was less certain, but, God, he felt better for a drink. Couple of beers first, just to irrigate the hangover. Then maybe a Bell's. And a bit of wine with lunch. That should sort him out.

Across the mêlée of salesmen, who were all drinking as if alcohol was an endangered species, he could see his quarry. But the murderer was surrounded and preoccupied. The confrontation would have to wait.

IT FINALLY OCCURRED in the afternoon tea-break, after the Biscuits and Cereals presentation.

Difficult to say exactly how well this extravaganza had gone. Robin Pritchard's initial remark had been predictable, and lulled those of the audience who'd managed to get back after lunch into the somnolent assurance that the rest of the programme would be equally bland. Legs were stretched out under the chairs in front, and eyelids drooped as the salesmen saw an opportunity to catch up on the sleep they had lost the night before and the sleep they would undoubtedly lose after the forthcoming banquet.

The outlining of the proposed ad campaign for the new Delmoleen muesli bar raised a flicker of interest, but none of the salesmen was prepared for the sudden change of gear from commerce to showbiz that followed.

Robin Pritchard made the most of the occasion. Suddenly raising his voice and adding to it a phoney ringmaster's razzmatazz, he shouted, 'But don't take my word for it! No, for the latest, mind-stretching news about the Delmoleen "Green", let me hand you over to—THE GREEN MACHINE!'

The appearance of a thickening green-bow-tied night-club singer in a green tuxedo, escorted by two male dancers in green waistcoats and two female dancers in green catsuits, certainly had the effect of waking the audience up, if only because it was such an unfamiliar sight at a Delmoleen sales conference.

But whether what ensued had the effect of exciting the salesmen about the new product they would shortly have to sell was less certain.

It undoubtedly excited them to laughter.

The performers had put in more rehearsal during the day and were now quite slick. The singer had added a few more sexy hip-gyrations in what he imagined to be the style of Tom Jones, but these elicited only coarse comments from the predominantly male audience.

This ribaldry was exacerbated by the actions of the female dancers. The prop they had been missing on the previous evening—the six-foot green-wrapped giant muesli bar—was held upright by the 'boys' at one point in the routine and caressed lovingly by the two 'girls'. Though the intention of these movements had not been erotic, the effect undoubtedly was. The Delmoleen sales force was an audience highly attuned to the detection of innuendo, and the phallic implications were not lost on them.

'Ooh, lovely! Do it some more!' came a throaty cry from the auditorium at the height of the female dancers' ministrations. This unfortunately got the girls themselves giggling and so, while the singer struggled gamely on, thrusting out his hips and extolling the *'Green—"Green"—Del—mo—leen'*, the chorus behind him had degenerated into something of a shambles.

Whether or not the sales force got the message about all the virtues of the Delmoleen 'Green,' there was certainly no danger that they would forget the name of the product.

So maybe the exercise hadn't been wasted, after all.

AT THE TEA-BREAK, Charles was in the Ambassador Hotel's reception area when he saw his quarry, on his own, going through into one of the lounges. At the bank of telephones in the recesses of the hall, Heather Routledge was hunched over a receiver, her tense body language leaving no doubt that she was once again talking to her mother.

'Oh, Mr Paris,' called the receptionist. 'There was another call from that Mr Skellern.'

'Thank you,' said Charles.

But he was not to be diverted, least of all by a call from Maurice. He went through into the lounge and sat in an armchair opposite his quarry, who was bent over the Top Table seating plan for the evening's banquet.'

'Afternoon, Ken.'

The Marketing Director looked up. 'Oh, Charles,' he acknowledged mildly, then grinned. 'Well, I remain to be convinced that Delmoleen sales conferences need to be converted into *The Black and White Minstrel Show*. Though, actually, on this afternoon's showing, it seemed more like *Oh! Calcutta!*'

Charles nodded. Ken Colebourne seemed fairly relaxed, or at least as relaxed as the responsibilities of the sales conference allowed him to be. It would be churlish to add another anxiety to his load at such a moment.

On the other hand, a human life had been taken. And, though, from what he'd heard of her character, he didn't have much respect for Dayna Richman, Charles Paris still had to find out the truth of what had happened to her.

'I want to talk about something a bit awkward, Ken . . .' he began gruffly.

'Oh yes? Problems?'

'You could say that. It's about Dayna.'

The name caught Ken Colebourne like a blow to the solar plexus. He gaped at his accuser, winded.

'I know about you having slept with her.'

'What!' The Marketing Director half-rose to his feet. 'For Christ's sake keep quiet about that! If Pat found out, it'd kill her!'

'I wasn't proposing to tell Pat.'

'Then what do you want? Are you after money too?'

Ken Colebourne's words satisfyingly confirmed Charles's conjecture. There had been an instant recognition of the subject under discussion, and no attempt at denial.

'No, I'm not after money.'

'Then what do you want? If you're offering moral judgement, I can do without it, thank you. I've punished myself quite enough for what happened. God, if you only knew how much I've regretted it, from the moment I did it—even while I was doing it. But things haven't been easy, with Pat being ill. I'm a normal man—God damn me for it—perhaps a bit over-sexed, I don't know—and that Dayna was a right little vamp. She knew what a man wants all right and—'

'I'm not blaming you for going to bed with her, Ken. I'm blaming you for what happened afterwards.'

'You should blame her for that, not me! I wasn't the one who taped the whole sordid business. I wasn't the one who introduced blackmail into the proceedings.'

'Did you ever get the tape, Ken?'

'No. I'm still not sure that it existed. She may have invented it, just to make her blackmail demands more forceful. Didn't really matter whether there was a tape or not. The threat of her telling Pat was quite sufficient. I'd have paid anything, I'd have done anything, to stop that happening.

'You don't know what it's been like for me with Pat these last few years . . . to watch someone you love, wasting away . . . all their life trickling through your fingers. And there's nothing you can do to stop it, nothing you can offer. Except love. So you go on telling them you love them, and then eventually that's all they've got. And the thought that some little tart could have threatened that love . . . Dayna seduced me when I was at a low ebb. It was nothing, just physical. But it would have killed Pat if she'd found out.'

'So you had to ensure that Pat never did find out?'

'I had to think of ways of doing that, yes.'

'And you confided in Brian Tressider?'

Ken nodded. That, thought Charles, made sense of some of the things Brenda had said the night before.

'Yes, I told Brian. We've always been mates, right from the start. I thought he might see some way out.'

'And did he?'

'Well, he ... he offered to help me with the money. Otherwise, he didn't really have any suggestions.'

'So you had to work out what to do on your own?'

The Marketing Director nodded. 'Yes. All kind of solutions went through my head. I hadn't really decided which one to go along with, when suddenly I had the most amazing piece of good luck ...'

But Charles was never to find out what that piece of good luck had been.

'Ken!' a controlled but tense voice hissed.

They looked up to see Brenda Tressider standing in the doorway. She was pale.

'Ken, Pat passed out while we were going round the winery.'

He was instantly on his feet. 'Oh, my God! Where is she now?'

'In your suite. I brought her back. She's conscious. She says she's fine. The hotel's organising a doctor.'

'I'll go straight up.' He turned to Charles. 'We'll finish this conversation some other time.'

In his face there was an expression of naked pleading. Do what you like, it seemed to say, do whatever's necessary, but please don't let Pat find out what happened.

After Ken had gone, the expression Brenda Tressider turned on Charles was very different. She had sensed what they'd been talking about.

And she despised Charles Paris for having been so insensitive as to raise the subject.

HE FELT FRUSTRATED AS, a few minutes later, he wandered back towards the main hall. To have been so near to a confession from Ken Colebourne and yet not to have got all the details...

A weariness filled him. What was the point, after all? Assuming what now seemed almost certain—that the Marketing Director had arranged the accident that killed Dayna Richman—what possible good would be served by bringing the man to justice for his crime?

All that that could achieve would be to deprive his dying wife of the comfort of a loving husband's presence during her last months.

And, weighing the moral claims of Patricia Colebourne against those of the late Dayna Richman... well, there wasn't much contest, really.

Charles felt low and depressed. He needed to talk to someone to reassure him. Frances? He glanced across towards the telephones. But no, it was term-time. Frances would still be at school, being responsible and headmistressly.

He caught the eye of Heather Routledge, who was still glued to the receiver. She raised her eyebrows in a despairing mime of the impossibility of getting off the phone.

'Charles. We need your help.'

It was Brian Tressider, tall, vigorous, reassuring. No one seeing him could have suspected the tragic deficiency that had blighted his married life.

'Yes? What can I do for you?'

'Look, Ken Colebourne's wife's ill—'

'I know. I heard from Brenda.'

'Right. Well, he's got to stay with her for the moment. But the thing is...' The Managing Director consulted his watch. 'Ken was about to do his marketing spiel for the sales force...'

'Oh. Yes.'

'You know how to use that autocue, don't you, Charles?'

THE BULK OF the presentation went fine. Charles hadn't been concentrating when Ken had rehearsed the day before, but he was enough of a professional to read a script unseen with a fair degree of competence.

And, though this time he was operating the slides himself, their cues were all clearly marked on the script that appeared magically on his invisible lectern. He held the control in his right hand and just clicked its button at the appropriate moment. He could see each new slide reflected in the glass of the control box at the back of the conference auditorium, and thereby check that he wasn't going out of sequence.

Of course, he didn't get much reaction, but then he hadn't expected much. Ken Colebourne's script didn't contain many jokes and, after the hilarity of the 'Green' song-and-dance act, the sales force were saving their laughter for Nicky Rules' cabaret later on.

It was very near the end of the presentation, when Charles was beginning to feel confident—perhaps even a little careless—that things started to come unstuck.

'And we still stand by the principles which made the company successful when it started,' he read from the autocue. 'We take pride in those principles. Everyone who works for Delmoleen knows that all our products are made by the most modern manufacturing methods...'

Nonchalantly, Charles pressed the control in his hand. It didn't seem to click. Hastily he pressed it again, and was surprised by a huge laugh from the audience.

He tried covertly to turn round. On the screen he could see the slide of the children in front of their rusty Caribbean hut and broken-down tractor. It didn't give the impression of 'the most modern manufacturing methods'. He had managed to get himself one slide out of synch.

Oh God, no. He could feel sweat trickling down his back as he pressed on through the script, desperately trying to regain control.

'They know the same high quality Delmoleen goods are sold all over the world... They know what the public think of Delmoleen.'

In the panic, his thumb slipped on the button. It clicked again. Reflected in the glass of the control box, he could see the screen with its screaming newspaper headline: '"THEY'RE RUBBISH! I'LL NEVER TOUCH ANYTHING THEY MANUFACTURE AGAIN!" SAYS BOTULISM BOY'S HEARTBREAK MOTHER.'

Once again the audience roared. They thought the 'Green' presentation was all they were going to get in the way of laughs that afternoon. This was a bonus.

Sweat prickled at Charles's temples. 'They know,' he floundered doggedly on, 'that the public trust the guarantee of hygiene that only comes from Delmoleen—and not from other companies I could mention. And they know that Delmoleen goods are sold at a price that's more than competitive. So they begin to understand what being a part of the Delmoleen family is really worth.'

Again his finger slipped on the control. The slide of bedtime drinks appeared, but all the cartons seemed to recede into background behind the huge sign reading '98p'. The audience's hilarity grew.

Head down and run for the line, thought Charles. Just get through it as quickly as possible.

'And, in these environmentally-conscious times,' he gabbled, 'they know that Delmoleen products are only made from the freshest of organically-grown natural ingredients. Yes, Delmoleen cares. Delmoleen is like a family. And I want to show you what sort of people are part of the Delmoleen family.'

Surely that was the final cue, wasn't it? He gave a despairing click on the control.

The screen behind him filled with a picture of vegetables.

The massed salesmen roared in uncontrollable hysteria.

Nicky Rules' cabaret was going to have to be bloody good to be funnier than this lot.

TWENTY-TWO

OF COURSE Brian Tressider brought them round. He
was a natural communicator, and he even managed to
give the impression that the farce of Charles Paris's
presentation had been in some way deliberate. He
charmed the sales force into a circle of complicity. He
motivated them. He made them feel excited—and even
privileged—to work for Delmoleen. It was a great
performance.

At the end he presented Daryl Fletcher with his Fiesta, which stood in gleaming splendour on a podium
at the back of the stage. The Top Salesman, grinning
hugely, made some derisively disparaging remarks
about his rivals, before taking the keys and posing for
cameras in the driving seat of his prize, with his Managing Director standing paternally beside him.

Daryl looked triumphant, but a little weary. Maybe
his participation in his wife's plans for the day had
taken it out of him.

And from the pride with which he surveyed his Fiesta, no one would have guessed he intended to trade
it in as soon as possible and spend the money on more
cosmetic surgery for his precious Cortina.

CHARLES HAD NOT expected to encounter Ken Colebourne again that evening, and was surprised to see
the Marketing Director hurrying through the crowded

bar towards him just before the banquet started. Ken
was neatly dressed in dinner suit and black tie. That
was the rule for the Top Table, though the assembled
salesmen were expected to wear what invitations, for
some reason, always call 'lounge suits'.

'How's Patricia?' asked Charles.

'Better, thank you. She's even insisting on coming
to the banquet.'

'That's good news, isn't it?'

Ken Colebourne looked uncertain. 'I hope so. She
says she feels fine, but it's always difficult to know
with her. She might just be doing it out of loyalty.
Anyway, she's not going to sit on the Top Table. She'll
be on a side one near the door, so if she does have to
leave, she can do so with the minimum of fuss.'

'Oh. Right.'

The Marketing Director hesitated. 'About what we
were discussing earlier . . .'

'Yes?'

'You got to keep quiet about it.'

'I will. I said I would.'

Charles suddenly felt the voluminous lapels of his
jacket seized as Ken Colebourne's face was thrust close
to his. He could smell the staleness of whisky on the
man's breath. 'You'd better!' the voice hissed. 'If I
find out you've breathed a word about it to anyone,
I'll bloody well kill you!'

Charles Paris realised, with a little shiver, that such
a threat, from someone who'd done what Ken Colebourne had done, had to be taken seriously.

THE BANQUET was more fun than he'd anticipated. The food was the predictable cardboard, but there was plenty of wine and the company was good. Charles sat with Will Parton, the Fletchers and a group of other rowdy salesmen and wives.

Since they had now discharged their obligations to the conference, the *Parton Parcel* team felt justified in getting quite drunk. Their contribution had been a success . . . well, probably a success. True, there was a slight question mark over the '*Green*, "*Green*"— *Del—mo—leen*' routine, but . . . No, it had been good, really good . . .

The more drinks they had, the more good they convinced themselves it had been, and they started to spin lucrative fantasies of all the new assignments *Parton Parcel* would take on, as the company rapidly cornered the market in corporate work.

Daryl and Shelley Fletcher also gave good value. He was flushed with success and alcohol, and she was flushed with something, too. Mercifully, Daryl was kept off the subject of custom cars as he engaged with his colleagues in a ribald exchange of jokes, to which Shelley contributed with many a throaty chuckle. She was a fine example for the success of the Equal Opportunity campaign, demonstrating a mind at least as filthy as any of the men's.

The atmosphere of the evening had about it a blokeishness of the kind Charles usually despised, but, well . . . once in a while it didn't hurt . . .

He looked round the crowded banqueting hall. At one of the side tables he could see Heather Routledge sitting beside Alan Hibbert. Neither seemed to be en-

joying their perk of being invited to the sales conference that much. They exchanged the odd word, but
maybe they had exhausted all their mutual topics of
conversation, working day by day in the warehouse at
Stenley Curton.

At another side table, Charles could see Patricia
Colebourne. She had been sat with a suitably mature
group of salesmen and wives, but conversation didn't
seem to be flowing there either. Nor was she eating,
just pushing the food round her plate with a fork.

She looked ghastly. Now almost transparently thin,
her skin had an unearthly sheen and her body swayed
slightly as if she might faint again at any moment.

Only the dogged set of her mouth showed the
strength of will that was holding her together. She was
determined to support her man. However ill she felt,
she would not allow anything to keep her away from
Ken's big night.

Charles glanced up at her husband on the raised Top
Table. He looked stressed and sweaty, as he tried to
concentrate on what the satin-tuxedoed smoothie beside him was saying.

This character Charles recognised to be Nicky
Rules. Though the game-show that had made this minor comedian into a national figure was not the kind
of programme Charles watched, the man's profile was
now so high that it was impossible not to recognise
him. The sharp nose and beady eyes were a regular
fixture on hoardings and magazine covers all over the
country.

Nicky Rules was *big*. It was quite a feather in Ken
Colebourne's cap to have booked him for the confer-

ence—however much Delmoleen had had to pay for the privilege. And, having heard the scale of money that even minor celebrities commanded for corporate appearances, Charles knew that Nicky Rules' fee would have been astronomical—certainly more for that one night than most of the salesmen present earned in a year.

Still, he was the right name to get. Daryl and Shelley Fletcher were very impressed. They loved his show. 'He's so rude, Chowss,' Shelley kept saying gleefully, 'so bloody rude to everyone. I wonder who he's going to get his knife into tonight . . . ?'

NICKY RULES had certainly done his homework.

He prided himself on tailoring his material to his audience. It wasn't that he came up with new jokes. By no means. Most of his jokes that night were of pensionable age, but each had been very carefully adapted to the Delmoleen set-up.

He started predictably enough. 'I was just talking to Brian, your Managing Director, about this conference. I asked him how many salesmen worked for Delmoleen. He said, "About half of them."'

The insulted salesmen roared their appreciation, confirming the old truth that audiences like jokes they recognise.

'Not of course that Brian himself has a problem about working. Never does anything else, does he? You know, he puts in such long hours in the office that on the rare occasions when he does get home, Brenda doesn't recognise him. Last time he walked into his house—and we're talking only six months ago—she called the police, said she got a prowler.'

This wasn't particularly funny, but it got the laughs. There was a kind of sycophantic recognition that the famous comedian had taken the trouble to find out about Delmoleen.

Nicky Rules knew how far he could go. Jokes about Brian Tressider being a workaholic were fine—in fact quite flattering. They bolstered his image, at the same time showing how sportingly he could take a joke against himself. But the comedian didn't risk any lines of a more personal nature against the Managing Director, certainly nothing that might hold him up to ridicule.

With other members of the management he was less charitable. He seemed to know who the safe butts were.

He homed in·on the ethnic origins of the Product Manager for Beverages. 'Paul Taggart's not really mean, you know. Mind you, couple of years back, he won a fortnight's holiday for two in the Seychelles. Left his wife at home and went by himself—twice!'

The Product Manager for Biscuits and Cereals did not escape unscathed either. 'Of course, Robin Pritchard went to business school, didn't he? Doesn't actually make him any more efficient, but at least he understands *why* he's inefficient!'

The butt of the joke smiled indulgently at this joshing.

'Did you know that he came to Delmoleen from an electrical goods company? Very high up the management he was there—used to go round selling vacuum cleaners!'

Robin Pritchard looked less amused by this.

'Went round to one lady's house, threw some dirt on the floor, said, "I have so much faith in my product that, if it doesn't clean up every speck of that dirt, I'll eat it off the carpet myself." Woman says, "Here's a spoon. We haven't got any electricity!"'

The audience found this very funny. Robin Pritchard smiled sourly, trying but failing to look as if he found it very funny too.

'And then, of course,' said Nicky Rules, 'there's your Marketing Director, Ken Colebourne...'

The comedian smiled his evil smile. 'Actually, you know, it's not the first time old Ken's been down to Brighton. Was here with his secretary a few weeks back to set the whole thing up—at least that was his story. When he got back to Stenley Curton, he said to his secretary, "Can you ever forget that lovely weekend we had in Brighton?" "Maybe," she said. "What's it worth?"'

The salesmen enjoyed this old joke, too. Ken Colebourne looked uneasy. But worse was to come.

'Of course, Ken's always had an eye for the young girls, hasn't he? When his wife got to forty, he said he wanted to change her for two twenties.'

Where Nicky Rules had got his information from, Charles didn't know. But what he said seemed to be striking a chord with the audience, so maybe Ken did have that kind of reputation round Delmoleen.

The comedian continued inexorably, 'Actually, Ken went up to one of the girls in the typing pool at Stenley Curton—said to her, "I dreamt about you last night." "Did you?" she said. "No," he replied, "you wouldn't let me."

'Then someone walked past his office and heard old Ken and one of the typists talking. "What are you trying to tell me?" she's saying. "I don't know," says Ken. "I'm groping for words." "Well," she said, "you won't find them down there."

'Story I heard about Ken taking on a new secretary. Really likes the look of her, he does. Says, "I'd like you to take the job. How much are you going to want to be paid?" "Hundred and fifty a week," she says. "Great," says Ken, "I'll give you that with pleasure." "Oh no," she says. "With pleasure it'll be two hundred and fifty!"'

How much longer Nicky Rules would have gone on in this vein, how much bluer he would have got, they never found out. Ken Colebourne had taken all he could take. He rose to his feet, kicked his chair back and strode off to the nearest exit.

Nicky Rules watched him go with a quizzical expression, then turned back to his audience.

'Apologies from the Marketing Director,' he said. 'Suddenly been taken randy.'

The audience roared and roared.

The mocking laughter rang in Charles's ears as he hurried off after Ken.

THE BANQUETING SUITE was in the basement of the Ambassador Hotel. Charles hurried out into the lobby and saw Ken Colebourne standing by the lifts, waiting impatiently.

The Marketing Director blazed a look of concentrated hatred at him.

'I didn't say a word,' Charles protested. 'I don't know what made him start off on all that stuff.'

'I can never face Pat again. Not after that.'

'Ken...'

Charles stepped forward, but Ken Colebourne was not to be comforted. He turned away, giving up hopes of the lift and pushing through the double doors that led to the stairs. As he turned, Charles caught the glint of a tear in his eye.

Charles followed through the doors, but his quarry was already out of sight. Must have been running flat out to get away so quickly.

Charles emerged by the reception area and hurried out through the hotel's main doors. There was no sign of Ken Colebourne on the rain-swept seafront.

Most likely gone up to his suite. Charles went back inside, had a cursory look in the lounges and bars of the ground floor, then walked up to Reception.

'Could you try Mr Colebourne's suite, please?'

'I think Mr Colebourne's involved in the Delmoleen banquet downstairs.'

'No, he just came out. Please.'

The girl checked a list and dialled the number. It was while the phone was ringing that Charles heard a commotion outside the front of the hotel.

Sickened by anticipation, he moved slowly towards the main door.

'I'm afraid there's no reply,' the receptionist called after him.

'No,' he murmured. 'There wouldn't be.'

The Ambassador Hotel is eight storeys high. On the eighth is a bar with panoramic views over the sea. It was to that bar, it emerged later, that Ken Colebourne had gone. He had ordered, paid for and quickly downed a large Scotch, then walked through the doors on to the balcony.

Hardly breaking his stride, he had climbed over the parapet, and jumped.

His body lay crumpled on the pavement directly in front of the hotel's main doors.

TWENTY-THREE

THE NEWS WAS smuggled discreetly to Brian Tressider, who, instantly decisive as ever, decreed that no purpose would be served by breaking up the party. So, showing no untoward emotion, he sat through the act of the American girl singer who'd been big in the charts in the early seventies, and then, when the band took over, began the first dance with Brenda in his arms. He subsequently did more public relations work, dancing jovially with the wives of specially favoured salesmen.

The official announcement of his Marketing Director's death would, he had decided, be made in the morning.

Charles Paris did not return to the banqueting suite. Instead, he went wearily to his room and ordered another Room Service bottle of whisky. They didn't have Bell's but he made do.

The death seemed so unnecessary, and he couldn't totally eradicate a feeling of guilt. Though he deserved no blame for the hideous inappropriateness—or perhaps appropriateness—of Nicky Rules' routine, Charles still felt responsible for having hounded the dead man earlier in the day. It wasn't a good feeling.

He didn't know how long he'd been sitting there, but about a third of the whisky had gone, when there was a gentle tap on his door.

'Come in,' he said, too dispirited to move.

It was Brenda Tressider, still immaculate in her ball dress. He shambled to his feet. 'Come in. Can I get you something? More of the tap water?'

'No, thank you.' She closed the door and moved a few steps into the room. 'I just wanted to say that I'm sorry about what happened . . .'

'Yes.'

'And that you mustn't feel bad about it.'

'Easily said.'

'Ken was devoted to Pat. He really couldn't have lived without her.'

'No, but they'd have got over this. They could have been reconciled.'

Brenda Tressider looked at him in puzzlement. 'What do you mean? They could have got over it? You know that Pat's dead, don't you?'

'What?'

'She felt ill during the banquet and slipped away without any fuss. She managed to get up to their suite, but there . . . she must have passed out on the floor . . . maybe just died straight away. Nobody'll ever know for sure. The Hotel Manager found her after . . . after they'd found Ken.'

'But—'

'She was very ill. This had been on the cards for a long time. And I'd always been afraid of how Ken would react when the moment finally came.'

'Oh. So what exactly do you think happened?'

'Ken must've noticed she was missing from her table. In the middle of the cabaret. That must be why he left in such a hurry. Then, when he got to their suite, he found her dead and . . . just couldn't go on.'

'Tell me, was Patricia present for any of Nicky Rules' routine?'

'No. According to the people at her table, she left before the coffee.'

So Patricia Colebourne had never even been aware of the suggestions that her husband was so afraid of her hearing. She had died in full confidence of his undivided love.

Brenda Tressider's reading of the events had not been the correct one. But it was, in its own way, tidy.

And it probably made a more satisfactory ending to the tragedy of Ken and Patricia Colebourne than the truth would have done.

TWENTY-FOUR

CHARLES PARIS FELT exhausted as he crossed the hotel's main lobby on the way to breakfast the following morning. The area was full of luggage and salesmen who were making an early start back to their scattered regions, hopefully re-energised by the previous two days, ready to return to the fray, to sell, sell, sell and increase Delmoleen's precious share of the foodstuffs market.

They didn't look very re-energised. 'Bleary' and 'hungover' would have been better descriptions. And the way some of them snapped at their wives suggested tempers had been shortened by the excesses of the night before.

Predictably enough, in the background Heather Routledge was talking on the telephone—or, more accurately, listening to the telephone. She had the receiver tucked under her chin, leaving both hands free to sort through some files which she was packing into a briefcase. Long practice had taught her that, as when listening to the radio, it was possible to do other things while her mother was talking on the telephone.

Charles found Will at breakfast, looking as ropy as he felt. 'How did your evening pan out?' Charles asked, as he sat down.

'Tiring. Ended up with the Top Salesman and his wife.'

'Oh, Daryl and Shelley? Yes, well, that could have been tiring.'

Will groaned. 'Certainly was.'

'Just the three of you? Or others?'

'Oh, bunch of other people came and went. God, one of the most exhausting nights I've ever spent.'

'Well, you're not getting any younger, Will. Can't go at it in quite the way you used to.'

The writer looked up curiously from his scrambled eggs. 'Go at what?'

'Sex.'

'Sex? There wasn't any sex involved, Charles.'

'Oh. Then what was it that was so exhausting?'

'What was so exhausting was listening to bloody Daryl telling me about all the exciting things he's done to his flaming Cortina!'

'Ah. Yes. Right.'

Charles's coffee arrived. That was welcome. The kipper, however, didn't seem such a good idea as it had when he'd ordered it.

'You heard about Ken Colebourne, Will . . . ?'

'Yes. Bloody tragic.'

'I agree.'

'Well, it means the one authentic Delmoleen contact I've got for *Parton Parcel*'s just gone out the window.'

Charles winced. That could have been more happily phrased.

'Have to see who the new Marketing Director is, and start the cultivating process all over again.'

'Hm. Still, at least it does mean I've got a solution to my mystery.'

'Mystery?' It took a moment for Will's fuddled mind to catch on. 'Oh, you mean your *murder* mystery. You still harping on that, are you?'

'Oh yes.'

'God, I thought you'd forgotten all about the idea.'

'By no means. No, I now know that a murder definitely took place, I know why, and I know who the murderer was.'

'All right then, surprise me, clever clogs.'

'What do you mean?'

'Well, tell me whodunit.'

'But it's obvious. I thought you'd gathered that.'

'No. I hadn't. Go on then—who're we talking about?'

'Well, obviously—Ken Colebourne.'

'Ken Colebourne.' Will was silent for a moment. 'We are talking about the same murder, aren't we? The girl Dayna in the warehouse . . . ?'

'Yes.'

'Who was crushed by the forklift truck—or rather by the pallets pushed by the forklift truck—during that lunch-break when we were making the video . . . ?'

'Yes.'

'And you think Ken Colebourne did it?'

'I'm certain.'

'Well, you're wrong, Charles.'

'I'm not wrong. I can't be wrong.'

'Oh, everyone can be wrong, Charles. Even you.'

'But—'

Will Parton spelled it out. 'During that lunchtime, you may recall, Griff Merricks and I and the rest of the

crew were invited to the Executive dining room. And
you weren't because you were improperly dressed.'

'I'm hardly likely to forget that.'

'No. Well, we were escorted to the Executive dining
room by Ken Colebourne. He sat with us right through
the meal.'

'But—'

'He only left when he was summoned by a phone
call announcing that there had been an accident in the
warehouse. I'm sorry, Charles, but your murderer had
a perfect alibi for the time of the murder—and I
should know, because I am that alibi.'

Charles Paris was totally deflated. In the Deflation
Olympics he would have defeated all comers, even
pancakes. 'Oh,' he said feebly.

'So sorry to be a spoilsport, love, but I'm afraid
you've got to start thinking of another perpetrator for
your precious murder.'

And even as Will said the words, Charles did think
of another perpetrator.

A woman. A woman who was in love with Brian
Tressider.

THEY SAT OPPOSITE each other in an otherwise empty
lounge. She had her coat on, ready to leave the hotel.

'I know exactly what happened that day,' said
Charles.

'Oh yes?' She remained cool, unruffled by his accusation. 'Tell me.'

'It was Dayna's boasting that signed her death war-
rant. She made no secret of her ambitions. She intended to use her sexual charms to make her way up

the company. That didn't worry you particularly one way or the other. It was only when she set her sights on Brian that you really saw red.'

'Perhaps.'

'And when you heard that she was going to start working in London.'

That did produce a reaction. A slight indrawing of breath. 'Yes. Yes, that was what did it.'

'Because it was history repeating itself, wasn't it?'

'Yes,' said Heather.

'You'd known Brian from the time you started working at Stenley Curton. He rose up the management ladder and was going to be transferred to London...'

She nodded.

'And at the same time you also had the offer of a job in London...'

'Yes,' she murmured.

'And you were all set to take it, all set to make the break from your family, to start your own independent life, to be near Brian, maybe see how things worked out between you...when your father died.'

'Exactly.'

'I can't imagine your mother was ever an easy woman, Heather...'

'No, she wasn't.'

'But, with your father's death, she started making even greater emotional demands on you.'

'You could say that, yes. In fact, from that moment she trapped me completely. She saw to it that I would never get away from her. Even when she dies, I'll still be trapped. There's not enough of my life left for me to do anything useful with it. Assuming that I had the will to do anything, anyway.'

'So you stayed in Stenley Curton. You monitored Brian's progress from a distance. Then, after a while, you heard he was going to get married.'

'Yes, I cried for weeks when I heard that. I've got reconciled to it, of course. Brenda's the right sort of woman for someone in his position. But, even now, I occasionally have unworthy thoughts about them. Like, for instance, I sometimes get an evil satisfaction from the fact that they don't have children.'

You might be surprised to know what else they don't have, thought Charles.

'But no, it was right. If Brian was going to get to the top, he needed a kind of social leg-up, and that was what Brenda supplied for him. She was at least the right class.'

'Unlike Dayna . . .'

'Dayna was just a common little scrubber. For her even to think she stood a chance with Brian . . . well, it was disgusting.'

'Yes. Killing her was a spur-of-the-moment thing, wasn't it, Heather?'

The woman nodded. 'She'd just been in my office, doing all her usual stuff, crowing about the job she'd got in London, crowing about her power over men. That's what I couldn't stand—the way she talked to me about sex . . . as if it had nothing to do with me . . . as if I didn't have any kind of sexual identity of my own . . .

'Anyway, that got me furious, but I certainly wasn't contemplating murder. And then my mother rang.

And I answered the phone and Dayna left the office. But, as she went out, she said something that implied that she had a video tape of her with someone high up in the Delmoleen management...of them, you know, making love...'

'And you thought she meant Brian?'

Heather nodded. Charles could envisage the scene. He was now coming round to the view that Dayna never had had any video of herself with Ken Colebourne. She had seduced him into her bed, yes, but there had been no camera running. That had all been bluff.

Still, she needed something to convince him that it was for real, and thought of Trevor's little cache of pornography. If Ken made any demur about paying her and needed frightening, well, maybe playing him a carefully chosen moment from one of Trevor's tapes might show she meant business.

'I should've realised earlier, Heather, that you've got very adept at doing other things while your mother's talking on the telephone. That day, you left her wittering on, and went through into the warehouse. You hadn't made any plans. Maybe you just intended to reason with Dayna, something like that. But then you saw where she was, scrabbling behind the pallets. And you saw that the forklift engine was running...'

'Yes. I couldn't think why it was.'

'You have Trevor to thank for that...for reasons that aren't important. So it was easy enough to push the truck into gear, pull down some cartons to make it look accidental and...leave things to take their course. Then back into your office, to find your mother continuing her monologue, unaware that you hadn't heard the last few minutes of it.'

'It's not as if I don't know everything she has to say by heart, anyway,' said Heather with sudden viciousness. 'God, she's a cow!'

Charles tended to agree with this assessment, but didn't comment. 'I've been rather slow, actually. I should have realised earlier. Really, from the moment that you gave Trevor an alibi.'

'That was a spur-of-the-moment thing, too. I didn't want there to be any sort of investigation, so I thought, if I got him in the clear, then there wouldn't be.'

'Hm. What, of course, I should have realised was that, once Trevor's alibi was shot to pieces, yours was too. Or your alibi was only your mother at the end of a telephone line.'

Heather smiled. In some strange way, their conversation seemed to have gratified her. 'So, full marks, Charles Paris. You've worked out exactly how the crime was committed.'

'After a few false starts, yes,' he agreed wryly.

'And what do you propose to do about it now?'

'I don't know.'

'Are you going to turn me over to the police?'

'I don't really know what that would achieve.'

'Justice would be seen to be done.'

'Yes, but... Justice in the abstract is a fairly meaningless concept.'

'Not everyone would agree with you on that.'

'Maybe not, but... I don't know. Obviously the death of any human being is a kind of tragedy, but nothing I've heard about Dayna Richman suggests to me that she was any great loss. If I thought your killing her was something rational and premeditated, I'd feel very differently. As it is... I find it odd to hear myself saying this, but her death really doesn't worry me that much.'

'Ah.'

'What about you? Does it worry you?'

'Surprisingly little. In fact, from the moment it happened, I've hardly thought about her death at all.'

An unexpected smile irradiated her face. For a second, she looked almost beautiful. The idea of her as a partner for Brian Tressider did not, at that moment, seem incongruous.

Charles sighed. 'And when I come to think of it, I really don't know what purpose would be served by your going to prison.'

'What do you mean—going to prison?' Heather burst out with sudden venom. 'Don't you understand—I've been in prison for the last twenty-seven years!'

'Yes,' said Charles Paris. 'Yes, I understand.'

There was a silence. Heather toyed for a moment with the handle of her bag. Then she rose to her feet. The brief moment of beauty was past. She looked what she was—an awkward, middle-aged spinster.

'I must go and ring her,' she said.

TWENTY-FIVE

PARTON PARCEL didn't, as it transpired, corner the market in corporate work. As the recession deepened, corporate budgets were cut back, and the reduced number of contracts that were around went to more established companies.

Anyway, Will Parton got commissioned to write some television scripts about an English detective and an Australian detective doing a year's job-swap. The series was, needless to say, being coproduced with an Australian company, and episodes were to be shot alternately in London and Sydney.

Will cursed his luck, complaining that the commission meant he'd have to put off getting down to his stage play. Still, the bills have to be paid, he said hopelessly, before settling down with relish to begin work on the first script.

For Charles Paris, the work vacuum was not so quickly filled. Indeed, what he'd thought of as his worst year ever looked like being superseded in the badness stakes by the next one. Maurice Skellern said in all his years in the business he'd never known it so quiet.

The agent, incidentally, did find out about the corporate work and was very aggrieved by what he saw as his client 'going behind his back'. Charles, retrospectively and apologetically, paid Maurice 15 per cent of what he'd earned from Delmoleen. What really annoyed him was that while he did so, he actually felt guilty.

Charles kept meaning to contact Frances, but kept putting it off. He thought, after their last encounter, it might be as well to cool things down for a while. Wait until another nice entertainment she'd really like to go to came up. The trouble was, now he'd lost his contacts in the corporate world, invitations to such events seemed to have dried up.

In fact, at times it seemed to Charles Paris that the only lasting thing he'd gained from his corporate experience was the suit. That remained in his Hereford Road bedsitter, on a hanger in the curtained alcove that served as a wardrobe. It hung next to his former suit, the model it had superseded. And with the passage of time, as if by some kind of osmosis of contiguity, it became as defiantly unfashionable as its predecessor.

Delmoleen, under the continuingly vigorous leadership of Brian Tressider, rode the recession better than many of its competitors. His wife, Brenda, continued in her professional role as a tower of strength.

Daryl Fletcher ceased to be a salesman and joined the Marketing Department at Delmoleen, where he was widely tipped to take over as Marketing Director when the current incumbent, Paul Taggart, retired. Daryl replaced the existing wheels on his Cortina with Firestones on Compomotive 3-piece rims and added some really rad graphics.

His wife Shelley got pregnant. Which was what she'd always wanted to do. She settled down to have lots of babies.

Robin Pritchard got head-hunted and joined another company as Product Manager for a revolutionary new ladies' depilatory, whose outreach was destined to be '*global*'.

Which was just as well, really, because he'd left the company before the failure of the Delmoleen 'Green' launch.

In spite of the findings of test-marketing, the public did not take to the product. For one thing, they were sick to death of muesli bars. For another, they were also sick to death of being told that things they bought were 'environment-friendly'.

Mainly, though, they just didn't like the taste. There was a pretty general consensus that the Delmoleen 'Green' had the flavour and consistency of a tablemat.

Also, the buying public just didn't yet appear to be ready for the concept of a *green* muesli bar. According to retailers, a lot of purchasers had brought their Delmoleen 'Greens' back, complaining they were mouldy.

CHASING AWAY THE DEVIL

THE DEVIL

A MILT KOVAK MYSTERY

First Time in Paperback

SUSAN ROGERS COOPER

HEAVEN CAN WAIT

On Friday night, Sheriff Milt Kovak of Prophesy County, Oklahoma, proposed to his longtime ladylove, Glenda Sue. She turned him down. On Saturday morning, Glenda Sue is found brutally murdered.

Kovak begins a desperate search to find the killer, well aware he's a suspect himself. When he discovers a first-class, one-way ticket to Paris in Glenda Sue's belongings, it's pretty clear she had been keeping secrets—deadly secrets.

"Milt is a delightful narrator, both bemused and acerbic."
—Publishers Weekly

Available in October at your favorite retail stores.

COFFIN
AND THE
PAPER MAN

Gwendoline Butler

First Time in Paperback

A
JOHN
COFFIN
MYSTERY

A PROMISE OF DELIVERY

Sixteen-year-old Anna Mary Kinver is raped and stabbed in the dank Rope Alley section of Leathergate. A former psychiatric patient, covered with blood, is picked up for questioning and subsequently let go.

Soon thereafter, John Coffin, chief commander of the Docklands district, receives the first in a series of notes from an anonymous letter writer calling himself "the Paper Man," who promises more bodies if Anna Mary's killer is not caught.

As the case goes unsolved, more bodies turn up. Who is the Paper Man?

"Coffin...solves a complex puzzle in this richly textured police procedural."
—*Kirkus Reviews*

Available in December at your favorite retail stores.

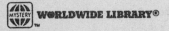

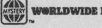

A DEB RALSTON MYSTERY

HACKER

First
Time in
Paperback

 LEE MARTIN

OVERKILL

Hovering perilously near burnout with the demands of
police duty and family life—specifically toddler, husband,
teenager and a friend comatose from a hit-and-run—Fort
Worth detective Deb Ralston now adds a grisly ax murder to her twenty-five-hour days.

A man and his computer are hacked to pieces. Eric
Huffman had no enemies, no reason to be so violently
murdered. The evidence is thin, but disturbing...since the
pattern seems poised to repeat itself in Deb's own house-
hold.

**"Martin continues the fine work begun in the earlier
Deficit Ending and *The Mensa Murders*..."** —*Booklist*

Available in January at your favorite retail stores.